The Monroe Sisters

NEED YOU NOW

ALIYAH BURKE

Need You Now
ISBN # 978-1-78686-346-1
©Copyright Aliyah Burke 2018
Cover Art by Posh Gosh ©Copyright February 2018
Interior text design by Claire Siemaszkiewicz
Totally Bound Publishing

NEED YOU NOW

Dedication

Thank you as always to Totally Bound for taking one of my stories. To my readers, I hope you enjoy these sisters. To DH, after all these years, what more can I say other than I love you more every day.

Chapter One

"Sometimes, you just need some dick."

Eva snorted, the margarita burning her nose as it exited, making her cough and her eyes water. "Did you just—oh, never mind, of course you did." She glared across the table at her sister with the vulgar mouth, Tara, as she accepted the napkin handed to her from the third member of the group. She wiped her lips before she dabbed at the corners of her eyes, hoping this incident hadn't turned her into a damn raccoon with how her makeup was running.

"What?" Tara blinked her almond-shaped black eyes, appearing unconcerned with her statement and how loud she'd made it. "It's true, a good fuck can go a long way." She sipped her Chardonnay and gestured to their other sister, Shai. "Tell her. I mean, she's a doctor. You'd think she would be aware of the benefits." Tara flipped her braid back over her shoulder, the pink streak in it vibrant and outgoing, much like the woman herself.

Shai drained the rest of her extra-dirty martini and put the glass down. "Tara's correct. You need to get laid. All of us do." She gestured for another drink.

Eva shook her head. She was the eldest and these two knew how to test her. "How did we go from my day to talking about a hookup?"

"Because your day didn't include one." Tara toasted her.

She sighed dramatically. *I highly doubt yours did either, Tara.* "That would be your logic. And just for the record, counselor, I'm a surgeon, not a regular doctor."

"Pretty sure there's a fucking MD after your name and I've seen you put DR in front of it. Or so it was the last time I saw you sign something."

Glaring at Shai, she huffed with as much indignation as she could manage to pull off having just choked on a drink moments prior. "No one asked for your opinion, professor."

"That's why I gave it. I am a professor. I interject when all the facts aren't present. I'm an educator." Shai flashed a grin, her white teeth stark against her smooth nut-brown skin.

"Why do I agree to come out with you two?"

"Because we're family and you love us," they responded in tandem.

"Ask me later about the love bit," Eva retorted as she gazed around the table.

Shai, the baby of the family, was the youngest tenured professor at the university. Eva's parents had adopted her when she was only six months old. Tara had joined the family at age two and held the middle-child distinction. All three of them were thick as thieves.

Running a hand over her spike cut, she spied a guy standing by the bar, eyes on the three of them. Her heart kicked up a few notches as recognition set in, but she couldn't pull from her memory banks just where she knew him from.

"Who's McHottie?"

"What?" she asked Shai.

"Which barfly are you staring at?"

"None."

"The witness is becoming hostile. I believe I should press the point," Tara added.

Eva faced her sister and muttered, "Bitch."

"Later," Shai said. "I've been thinking about what was said earlier."

Eva glanced over at her, eyebrows up in silent question.

"You know, about you not getting any cock."

She covered her eyes. "This is the problem — well, one of the problems — with having a professor and an ADA as siblings, you two are used to having to yell. There is something called an inside voice. You know, where you talk quieter, so the entire bar doesn't learn about me not having sex lately?"

"Because that was stated so eloquently and with your inside voice." Shai's tone dripped with humor.

Lord, could the floor just swallow me up? She met the amber gaze of the man across the way.

From the way his bow-shaped lips had kicked up, he'd overheard the embarrassing exchange. He raised his beer in her direction.

"Focus, please."

Professor tone. That's what Eva called it. She'd heard Shai use it numerous times in her classes and it never failed to silence the noise even in an auditorium. However, her sibling had a way with people and could easily get them to listen to her. It was a gift.

"I need a refill for this," Eva groused, waving for another pink-grapefruit margarita. "Especially since the last bit wasn't enjoyed as it exited my nose."

Her sisters exchanged a look and she realized they'd already discussed this and were springing it on her, tag-team style. As they waited, however impatiently, she allowed her gaze to drift back across to where Amber Eyes stood talking with three other men, also good-looking, but none of them rang the bell of recognition for her. His eyes flickered in her direction more than once and she again scrambled to recall where she'd seen him before. He wasn't a random hookup, she didn't do those, but from the way he watched her, there had to be something she was missing.

"Here you go." The waiter set her drink in front of her and took away the empty.

She nodded her thanks and put her attention on her sisters.

Tara with her hot-pink bangs and the long stripe down along the right side of her glossy jet-black hair. Then her gaze flickered to Shai with her purple streak in her dark brown pixie cut. Yep, trouble in their eyes and sass on their lips.

"As I was saying," Shai began again, "we've all been insanely busy. I mean, even for us to get here tonight, we've had to reschedule this three times. Tara and I have already talked about this and we need to step up and take control of our sex lives. Or the lack of them, as the case has proven to be."

"I haven't found a guy I want." Eva rolled her eyes at the lie that poured from her mouth.

Guys led to things like thinking of the future, and that typically meant children, which was where she shut down. She was sterile. Would never have a child of her own the natural way. And while she told herself she'd come to terms with that fact, the truth was she hadn't. Nor was she ready to try to explain this to a man who she'd fallen for only to have him say no and rip her heart out all over again before stomping it into tiny smeared lumps of muscle.

Her siblings sneered in response, yanking her from the depressing dark hole she was falling into as if she'd stepped off a building to embrace gravity.

"It needs to happen for all of us," Tara took over. "We're professional women who are dedicated to our careers and have neglected ourselves. That's unacceptable. We don't have to give it up. Men find a way to do this, which means obviously so can we. This is what we came up with."

Shai nodded. "We each take a week from work. All the same week and pick a beach. We go there, have a room and find some stranger to fuck. A week-long one-night stand, so to speak."

"We're going to the same place?" Eva pushed the instant *no* from her mouth, her body jumping to life, waving its hands, demanding some one-on-one attention from a person of the male variety. Battery-operated machinery wasn't cutting it. Neither was the touch of her own fingers.

"Nope, different ones. If we were together, then we'd be together and wouldn't be getting laid." Tara moved her glass to the side and rested her elbows on the table.

"I can't just take time off," she protested.

Tara glared at her. "Neither can we, but we're planning ahead, so it's not just taking time off. It will be considered a vacation—something we are actually allowed to indulge in. Same week. Different locales. A week of hot, guilt-free, mind-numbing, leg-shaking, can't-move-a-muscle-after, sweaty-all-over kind of sex."

Eva couldn't deny how amazing that sounded. *So long as I can keep my internal commentary shut down about how great he may or may not be with a child.* Damn it, she wasn't supposed to go down this road. She lifted her drink. "Here's to us and our weeks."

"No more arguments?" Shai questioned with a raised eyebrow.

"Nope, you said it perfectly. We've put others before us for too long. Time to take the bull by the horns, so to speak." She drew her phone from her gold clutch. "Where are we each going and when? Different beaches, but same distance of travel? Like we all head to places in Mexico. That way, we can tell Mom and Dad we're taking a vacation together."

"Agreed." Tara's statement was followed within seconds by Shai's succinct one.

They had their phones in their hand moments later as they each picked a location.

* * * *

Puerto Vallarta

Eva shouldered her purse and walked off the plane. The sun shone bright through the airport windows, making even this place seem cheery. As she headed for baggage claim, she withdrew her cell phone and sent a text to her sisters, alerting them she'd landed fine.

She stood with the others and scanned the group waiting for their luggage to come. According to her sisters, all she had to do was pick the guy she wanted and go from there. *God, we should have done this before. I cannot wait to get this vacation started. Now, all I need is to find the right one.* Hell, it was like a candy store. *I pick whichever one I want. No harm, no foul. This is strictly about me and my need to get my world rocked. No strings, no fuss, no muss.*

It didn't take long to secure her luggage or grab a cab to the hotel. Bag on the oversized chair in the corner, she flung open the doors leading out to the balcony. Beyond the railing, the ocean beckoned. The Midwest just didn't have places like this. Not that she had an issue with where she lived...it just wasn't Puerto Vallarta. There were no sandy white beaches with a beautiful blue water outside her window, bringing the sounds of laughter and the scent of the ocean.

Her phone buzzed and she reached for it, smiling as she found a text from Tara.

Glad to hear it. Just pulling up to the gate now. Have fun and ride him hard.

She chuckled and replied with a smiley face. "I would love to ride him hard. Now, I just have to find him first." She opened her suitcase and tossed the phone to the king-sized bed. "That isn't going to happen if I'm keeping to myself in the room." Rooting through her clothing, she found her bikini. "So I need to get down to the sun." Once it lay on the bed spread, she reached for the first button on her white shirt.

After she'd changed, she checked her phone again. Still nothing from Shai, and that worried her, so she sent her another text. According to the itinerary, her sister should have landed already at her destination, and it wasn't like Shai not to send confirmation.

* * * *

The moment she walked into his line of sight, Grant Harrison was mesmerized. Her peach bikini made his dick rock-hard in seconds with how her suit curved around her figure. Tiny waist, toned muscles and a sway to her hips he couldn't manage to tear his gaze from. She carried a small beach bag, not huge and oversized like many of the tourists.

He slid off the stool, grabbed his drink and trailed her to the edge of the hotel bar as she stepped out onto the sand. She turned heads as she walked by to the water. Both men and women took in the view she offered. Drink finished, he followed the same path she took to the beautiful blue water.

His mysterious goddess walked along the edge, the water lapping over her feet. As he watched, she relaxed. He could see the stress in her melting away beneath the warm sun. While not as tan as a lot of the women, strolling practically nude, she still stole his breath.

Heated sand beneath his feet warmed his soles as he navigated to her side. Stopping there, he crossed his arms and glanced down at her. "Beautiful," he commented.

A smile quirked her lips. "Yes, gorgeous. Don't have views like this back home."

He didn't even lift his gaze from her curvaceous form. "Me either."

"I was talking about the ocean."

"Water is water in my opinion. It's what goes with it that makes it beautiful." He had no qualms about being caught staring at her. "Name's Grant."

She angled her body toward him and he dragged his eyes up the front of her bikini, swallowed hard, blinked to see her belly button again and did it once more. High on her hips, the top material dipped low over her chest, teasing him with smooth, pale skin. While not overly huge, her breasts filled out the top in a mouthwatering display of feminine perfection. The dark coral hue smashed into him as if he'd just ingested a plate of oysters and was more than ready to show how good his libido was.

"Eva. And where is home, Grant?"

Yes, her lips mesmerized him as well. "I travel quite a bit for my work, but for the moment, it's in Arizona. For you?"

"Quad Cities." She ran her gaze over him, her hunger spilling free. "An area covering Southeast Iowa and Northwest Illinois."

Christ, it had been a while for him if this was what his small talk amounted to. It shouldn't be this difficult. Not to make his intentions known and find out if she was receptive of them or not. He moved closer, the air between them sparking and charging. "And what do you do there?"

"Work," she said, her tongue flicking out to dampen her lips. She never took her eyes from him. "Too damn much."

He kept his gaze locked with hers. "Nothing more specific?"

She lifted her hand and settled it on his chest. "Are you here with someone?"

"Not other than you." His heart pounded and his dick swelled further. Christ, he was going to puncture his suit if he didn't get some relief soon.

"Wife?"

"Never. Husband?"

"Not yet." She splayed her fingers and moved them through his chest hair. "Are we going to stand here and discuss the ocean or go somewhere else?"

"Somewhere else. My room is right back there."

She never looked to where he pointed.

He snaked his arm around her waist and drew her flush to him, his cock pushing against her. "I've wanted to fuck you ever since I saw you walk by me."

She looped her arms around his neck, tongue peeking out to hit the corner of his mouth. "Don't hear me complaining, do you?"

He lifted her in his arms, wheeled around and strode back to the hotel, staring in her eyes the entire time. Even in the elevator, he didn't put her down. Not until they got into his room did he allow her feet to hit the floor. Then he kissed her.

Grant groaned at her taste, a mixture of coffee and mint. When she backed away, he let her, but he kept staring. Her lips turned up in a small smile as she reached behind her neck and pulled. The top of her bikini fell to the carpeted floor of his hotel room.

Holy shit.

With a sure push, the bottoms were around her ankles and she kicked them away.

He gulped some air as he ran his gaze over her once more. From the sapphire tips of her blonde spiked cut to the exposed creamy skin, she was damn near perfect. A landing strip of hair guided his sight to her core. The lips glistened and he knew she was ready for him and he'd not even touched her yet.

She took a step and closed the distance between them once more. "You seem a bit overdressed for what I have in mind. Let me help you." Bending close to kiss his bare chest, she worked her way down to his belly button.

"Wait." A guttural rasp slid from his mouth seconds before she pulled down his shorts. His cock, long and hard, sprung free, bobbing before her.

"Hello, gorgeous," she purred as she curled her fingers around his shaft.

He widened his stance, breathing faster and shallower. A few cursory pumps prior to when she flicked her tongue over the head.

A moan fell free from between his lips and he sank his hands into her hair. Closing his eyes ever so brief, he tried to control his urge just to thrust deep into her throat. Opening them, he peered down at her to discover she watched him in return with those dark blue eyes.

She never looked away as she blew him. Bobbing on his cock, she didn't allow any part of him to go unattended. From the sensitive head to his balls, she gave each their due.

Grant couldn't pull his gaze from her face. There was something amazing about watching a woman happily give head. When his balls drew tight against him, he lifted her from where she knelt before him and carried her to the bed. "Not yet," he said.

Her response was dragging her tongue along her lower lip.

He placed her down gently. His was cock so hard, it ached. "I don't have much patience right now. I really want to fuck you."

She lay back, legs slightly spread, and he settled beside her. "And we're back to, do you hear me complaining?" A smile. "Although, I have to say, I was enjoying your dick in my mouth."

His cock jerked at her words, then again, when she circled him once more with her touch. "Fuck this." He reached around her to the bedside table and dug in the drawer for a condom.

The moment he found and grabbed one, she took it from him. Eva rose onto her knees as she straddled him.

"Allow me." The rip of the packet was followed by her tossing it to the side. Eva took him in hand and rolled it down his length. She was up and over him, sinking down, taking him deep inside her body. "Oh, shit," she groaned.

Yeah, he was on par with that statement.

Hot. Tight. Wet.

He gulped and grabbed her hips with his hands.

She gazed down at him, bottom lip caught in her teeth. As he stared, she leaned forward and put her hands on his chest.

For a moment in time, they stayed like that, lost in each other's eyes. Connected in the most physically intimate of ways. He swore, there in that second, something more passed between them.

When she moved, any and all thought went out of his head.

Eva rode him. Undulating, rocking, and finding a rhythm she liked as she discovered her own release.

While it wasn't the easiest thing to do, Grant let her set the pace for now. As she fucked him, he swore there would be more. For whatever reason, he could see she needed to get an edge off.

Go ahead, baby, use me. Fuck me as you will, I'm fine with this arrangement, just know that I'll take mine when you're finished.

She closed her eyes and dropped her head back as she continued to guide him along this path she took toward release. Her nails dug into his flesh as she came around him with a cry.

Grant didn't mind the bite of pain, in fact, he rather liked it. But as soon as her slit began pulsing and clenching around him as she came, he rolled them over, putting her on the bottom.

"My turn," he rumbled against her lips.

She kept up with him, never once missing a beat. Hooking her legs behind his back, she drew him in as deep as he could go. He ground his jaw, determined not to give in yet. This was the sweetest pussy he'd been in, ever, and he didn't want to leave.

She didn't make it easy. Not with the way she tightened and flexed her internal muscles around him. She milked him and he couldn't last any longer.

With a low roar, he came hard. Thrusting fast and deep.

Sliding her arms around his shoulders, she pressed her face into him as he went balls-deep inside her. Her entire body shook and shuddered as they both came.

Grant nearly collapsed on her but rolled to the side at the last moment. He gathered Eva in his arms and together, limbs entwined, they let their racing hearts slow, breathing calm, and bodies relax.

"Damn," she muttered against him.

His lips twitched as he smiled. "Couldn't have said it better myself."

She trailed her fingers along his torso. "That took the edge off. I need some more."

A woman after his own heart. "I'm here to serve."

Eva bit at his nipple with light teasing snaps. "Good to hear."

Grant knew this was far from over.

Chapter Two

Eva stirred and looked around the darkened room. Correction…most of the space was dark. One lamp in the far corner was lit. She blinked a few times and tried to get her bearings.

What's to get? You found a man, rode him until you couldn't move and collapsed in bed with him. Mission accomplished. Truth be told, she wasn't sure she would be able to move now. She didn't want to, but she couldn't stay there.

Internal commentary notwithstanding, she agreed. This had gone according to plan, but now, she had to get back to her room. Shifting free of the strong arm holding her to him, she paused and glanced down at the man in bed with her.

Much taller than she, he easily stood six feet, his black hair combined in beautiful fashion with tanned skin and those light blue eyes that created a burn within her she wasn't sure he would have been able to put out. He did, and she was grateful, but damn, the whole experience had been amazing. His muscular body had no trouble holding her up against a wall while he fucked her.

It was a shame to sneak out, but she needed to check on her sister and make sure she got there okay. Sliding free of the bed, she glanced around the room, searching for her long-discarded bikini.

Of course, near the door where I dropped it like the slut I am. Eva moved slow, her muscles protesting the slightest movement. It sure as hell wasn't elegant — she'd call it more of the shuffle. And not the Ickey Shuffle either, more like a lame duck one. This man had worked her well, reminding her that she'd been lax in using all those muscles. She shimmed into the bottoms first then walked to where the top was and tied it on.

"Where are you sneaking off to?"

Damn, even his voice could make her wet. Deep and decadent, it reminded her of his touch and lord knew what that did to her. "I have to get to my room and check on my sisters." She faced him once she'd put on her layer of armor, puny though it may be.

"They're here?" He stretched and offered her another view of his naked chest.

"No, but I haven't heard from either of them yet and need to make sure they're both okay."

Grant sat upright with the sheet bunched at his waist. The light color of cotton stark against his tanned skin. "Anything I can do?"

"No, I just need to give them both a call and check to see if there are any messages."

He slid to the edge and put his feet on the floor. "You don't carry it with you in your bag?"

"I didn't want to disturb you."

"So after those hours of incredible sex we just shared, you think I'm going to be bothered or disturbed by you?"

Grant stood and her focus went directly to his dick. It took a bit for her to force herself to meet his gaze once more.

Eva licked her lips. "I don't know what to think." *Not entirely true, I'm thinking a lot about you being inside me.*

He moved toward her, drawing her gaze back to the erect cock standing out between his legs. She whimpered as more longing coursed through her.

"Think this. I want you to stay. I want you to sleep here with me. I want breakfast with you after and we can explore this town together."

"You sure you don't have plans that I would be getting in the way of?"

He paused in front of her and tipped her chin up to him. The light highlighted the shadowed scruff on his square jaw.

Something that she longed to touch, caress and kiss.

For starters.

She was seriously going to have to lock up her libido if she was going to figure out how to get through this without looking like some sex-starved addict.

Exactly what I am.

Maybe she could lock up her internal commentary right along with it.

He dipped his head and brushed their lips together before walking away and picking up her bag.

Eva turned and observed him as he did this. Fixated on the muscles in his ass. Christ, even those were impressive. Her mind flashed down the road they'd just gotten off together and she remembered digging her fingers into the flesh of his butt as he'd thrust into her, deep and hard.

With her stuff in one hand, he captured hers with the other and led her back to the bed, where he dropped her bag by the side. He climbed in and tugged her along. "Here you go, problem solved." Once they were back in bed, he put her beach sack next to her.

She dug for her phone in the bottom and her breath hitched as his fingers brushed along the back of her neck. His lips followed the same trail and she trembled as she pulled out the device.

"Do you want me to order something to eat?"

"No, thank you. I can wait until morning."

"Baby, it *is* morning. It's five."

"Oh, in that case, yes, please." She unlocked her phone and pulled up her messages. Nothing from Shai. Three unanswered from Tara, however, and she read them quickly. All the same thing. Had she heard from Shai?

Grant put the menu beside her and kissed her shoulder.

She could get on board with his insistence on being so tactile. Hell, she wanted to return the favor to him. Skimming it quickly, she pointed out what she would like.

As he called for their order, she called Tara.

Her sister answered on the second ring. "Have you heard from her? And why didn't you get back to me sooner?"

"Hello to you, too, Tara. No, I haven't heard from her and I just now got your messages." Unease filled her. "Are you okay?"

"Me?" Tara cleared her throat. "I'm fine, yes, fine."

Had she been alone she would have called her sister out on the hemming and hawing, but she wasn't, so she let it go for the moment. "Okay, I will try Shai once more and if I get in touch with her, I'll tell her to call you. If not, I'll send you a text and we can figure out how the fuck we're going to find out what's going on."

"I'll call the airline and see if her plane landed and if she'd gotten on. I will use the office to do so."

Now she knew her sister was worried about Shai, as she didn't use the DA's office for her own devices. So for her to say it without needing any prompting, Tara was scared.

"Let me call her once more. You sure you're okay, Tara?"

"I will be once I figure out what the hell is going on with my sister. What about you? Get some hot man to ride?"

She cut her gaze to the left where Grant was still placing their order. "Sure did. With him now."

A low whistle crossed the line. "Always knew you were part whore."

Eva smiled. "Learned all I know from you."

"Only works if you're not the eldest so sorry, we learned from you. I'm fine, as well, found a man. He's in the shower now, which is good because my cootchie needs a rest."

"Christ, Tara, I don't need to hear about your cootchie at all."

Grant looked at her with his lips turned up in a wicked grin.

Of course, he would have heard her big mouth blurt out that part. *Why can't I ever control my mouth when I'm talking to my sisters?* Heat raced up her cheeks. "I'm going now, and I'm going to try Shai once more. Keep me posted and have fun, Tara."

"You, too, Eva. Love you."

"I love you, too, sis. See you soon." She ended the call and immediately dialed Shai's number. It rang once, twice, three, four times, before it went to voicemail.

Eva made a fist and waited for the beep. "Shai, this is Eva. Where the fuck are you? We're worried sick about you. If you're with a man, stop fucking him long enough to call and let us know you're okay. If you need us, call and we'll be on the next flight to wherever. Christ, just call us. Love you." She dropped the phone on the mattress and worried her lower lip.

"Hey, everything okay?" Grant sat beside her, rubbing her arm.

"I don't know. My sister isn't picking up her phone."

"And that's not common?" He never looked away from her face, giving her all his attention.

"We, my sisters and I, planned simultaneous vacations. We each picked a beach in Mexico for a week. If we went to the same place we'd spend the time together and this was so we could have —"

"Sex."

She was too concerned about her sister to check the words she spoke. It didn't matter if she hurt his feelings. "Basically, a week-long booty call."

"Glad I made the cut." He moved back to the headboard and brought her with, tucking her close to him. "So, the one who hasn't landed? Or rather hasn't called yet?"

"Baby of the family. And it's not like her, she's not the typical baby of the family. She's a college professor. We're worried because we haven't heard anything from her. Our agreement was we send text messages when we landed and again when we made it to the hotel. Then once a day so we know all is fine."

"Okay, and we know the plane landed safely?"

"Tara is checking on that now," Eva answered as she texted her sister that she still hadn't reached Shai. "I can't help but fear the worst. And if that happens, I don't know what we're going to tell our parents."

"Told them you were all going together to the same place, did you?" He rubbed his foot along her leg.

"We just said Mexico. Never actually stated we were staying in the same place." God, she was really worried now. Her fears were racking up as each second passed her by. There had to be a better way to figure this out without freaking herself out.

"Don't get worked up. Let's see what's going on first. Perhaps there was a delay. Where was she going?"

"She booked a room in Cancun."

Her phone buzzed and she looked down at it.

Plane landed fine, she was on it. What now?

She didn't have a clue. "Her plane landed safely but now we're not sure what to do."

"Did you check your email?"

She looked at him, face scrunched up. "Why?"

He gave a slight shrug. "I hate to say it but maybe her phone was stolen. If you're like my sibling and myself, I don't have the number memorized, so I couldn't call either. But I do know email addresses."

Shit, she never thought of that.

Checking email, maybe she had her phone stolen.

A thumbs-up from Tara came back, and in the next moment, Eva was signing into her email account.

Sure enough. There was a message from Shai, addressed to them both.

Hey. So my phone was stolen at the airport by some lowlife motherfucker who I want to track down and beat six ways to Sunday. I've got a burner and this is the number, call me when you can. Having a blast otherwise. Love you both.

She dropped the phone and wrapped her arms around Grant tight. "Thank you so much for that."

"I take it there was good news?" He dropped a kiss on the top of her head. A knock at the door had him leaving the bed, tugging on his shorts, all prior to going to answer it.

"Yes."

"Hold on, I'll be right back."

Eva pressed the number into the phone and called while watching him stride out of the room. Something more was going on here, a deeper emotion she wasn't sure she was ready to delve into. One that involved issues and questions she promised herself would be off-limits on this vacation.

"Hello?"

Relief swarmed her at the slightly husky voice that poured over the line. "Shai? Thank God, I've been so worried."

"Sorry, Eva. I don't know how it happened. But, I'm fine."

"Do you need anything? Did they get anything else?"

"Nope, just my phone," she replied with a slight edge to her tone.

"What about your password? Can they crack it?"

"If so, they deserve to get into my phone."

"Christ, you put in some of that insanity stuff you teach, didn't you?"

"Well, I don't use the word fluffy, that's for sure."

Eva laughed, grateful to hear her sister's voice and know all was okay with her.

"Now, tell me, did you find a man?"

"Christ, Shai, I've been worried about you and you want to know if I found a man to hook up with?"

"We each have our own concerns."

"You're such a crazy person. Yes, I did. In fact, he's getting our breakfast now."

"Ohh, already spending the night, you slut."

Eva smiled, more than happy to be considered Grant's slut for the little while she was down here. "Trying to live up to your expectations."

Shai laughed. "You surpass it, always. I have another call coming in and I'm going to guess this is Tara. I'll text you later, now that I have your number. Have fun, sis. Love you."

Eva leaned back and exhaled heavily. The amount of relief she felt, she couldn't begin to express. It would be a lie to think she'd not panicked about what to tell their parents or when she wondered if she'd ever see her sister again. Most of the time yes, she was levelheaded, but when it came to her family, there were times that just wasn't the case. When that one sister was in a foreign country and she was unable to get ahold of her, yes, it made her less than stable.

"Breakfast is served," Grant said, wheeling a cart into the bedroom.

"Good, I'm starved."

"Everything okay?"

"Fine, thank you." She watched him approach with the cart and couldn't help but feel mushy over the fact he was bringing her breakfast in bed. *Do people get more than just friendship vibes in such a short time? Because I'm sitting here imagining him doing this for the rest of our lives.*

* * * *

Grant observed Eva as she played volleyball with a group of people on the beach. He sat on a towel and watched them play with a smile on his face.

His vixen was a tomboy in disguise. Her competitive streak was blatant as she shouted at her fellow teammates to work harder and not to lose to the other team. Today her bikini matched the tips in her hair, a rich sapphire blue. She played bigger than she was. By far the shortest person out there, it didn't stop her in the least as she set up shots for others or went in for the dig.

After a raucous game, eventually her side won, and she waved off the offer to play once more, instead trekking across the brilliant sand to where he waited. Plopping down beside him with a grunt, Eva took his drink and guzzled it. "Damn, I'm thirsty," she announced the obvious when she came up for air.

"Apparently." He touched the blue tips of her hair, smoothing the silken strands through his fingers. There wasn't any way for him to describe how he enjoyed being with her and more than just in a sexual way.

She shoved the bottle back in his direction and reached for her bag, rooting through it. "That was good, I needed that. Thanks for hanging out while I took in a game."

Grant dragged a finger along the back of her neck, pleased with the slight tremble she exhibited. "No problem, it's not like watching women play beach volleyball is exactly a hardship here."

"Suppose not." She pulled out her phone and checked it.

He understood what she was doing, checking in with her sisters. That first night, he could taste her fear it had been so thick. Now, he wouldn't begrudge her anything when it came to making sure they were safe. He would do the same thing if it were his sister.

When she finished, she leaned back on her elbows.

He unabashedly ran his gaze over her form. They'd spent all the time here together and he meant *together*. His room, her room. It didn't matter. They explored together, swam and slept the same way. He didn't think he'd ever get enough. He hoped it would continue for the rest of their week.

She mesmerized him and he hadn't figured out why. Yet. He was trying. There were times when a connection was formed, but it was more than that. He hadn't been with her very long and he was already imagining a future with her. Somehow, he knew she was his one. "What's next?" he asked, reclining beside her.

"I could use a break. Just chill out in the shade and enjoy a cold drink."

"You feeling okay?"

"Fine, just tired. Someone kept me up late last night." She shot him a sly glance. "And this morning."

He laughed. "So they did. Okay, then, let's go."

He picked up the towels and draped them over his shoulder as she grabbed her bag that held their key cards. As they walked, Grant reached out and captured her hand, smiling when she allowed him to lace their fingers.

Back in the hotel, they went to her room and shared a shower. After which they took a nap on the bed.

He woke first and lay there watching her sleep. On her back, one arm over her eyes, the white sheet barely covering the mounds of her breasts. His mouth watered and he wanted to tug it down and give himself another taste, but he didn't. Instead, he got up and dressed, then went downstairs to order them both a drink.

As he rode back up on the elevator, he thought about his time with this woman.

I don't really know all that much about her. I know what she likes in bed, that she's a screamer. She loves being on top and taken from behind. But I don't have a damn clue about the rest of her. Haven't even seen a picture of her family and I know next to nothing about her life.

Grant stepped off the elevator and made his way to the room. This not knowing bothered him. Sure, it had only been a short time for the both of them, but he felt something real for her. Something he'd like to continue when they headed back to the States.

Juggling the drinks, he unlocked the door and pushed into the room.

"Oh, God…"

A moan reached him. He paused, allowing the door to close behind him. Cocking his head to the side, he checked to make sure there wasn't anyone in the room who shouldn't be there. Nothing… He went to the bed and almost dropped the drinks.

Eva lay there on top of the bedding, eyes closed, head thrown back, as she fingered herself. Her other hand teased her breasts, tugging on her nipples.

He stared at her, plunging her digits deep into her wetness as her thumb worked her clit. Putting the drinks down on the stand by the television, he moved to the bed. "I see I missed the party."

"Not missed," she panted, opening her eyes to stare at him, lust overflowing them. "Just late."

God, she wasn't even embarrassed to have been caught masturbating. He loved a woman who owned her sexuality. His dick pressed hard against the material of his shorts, tenting it out. "Let me join in then."

Eva removed her fingers and held them out to him. Grant bent at the waist and eagerly sucked them into his mouth while he tugged off his shorts. He loved her flavor, a honeyed spice. Curling his tongue around her two fingers, he got all the cream he could, then nipped the ends.

Widening her legs more, Grant turned her toward him, sank between them, knees on the floor. Her heady scent floated to his nose and he wanted just to indulge, but he took his time. He spread her lips more and ran his tongue up along the edges, avoiding any contact with her clit.

"Oh, hell," she cried out, bucking her hips, rubbing her wetness on him.

He teased her with rapid laps of his tongue, pushing it deep into her but never touching her clit. Grant wouldn't let her put her hand back there either when she tried to stimulate the nub.

"My turn," he said. "You had your chance to play. Now, it's mine."

"Grant."

He smiled briefly at the sexual frustration in her tone but didn't change what he was doing. He inched them

Need You Now

back until he rested on his heels and dragged her legs over his shoulders, so she couldn't shut them.

As he blew on her clit, she squirmed in an attempt for more contact. He slid two fingers inside her and began thrusting. Her pussy clamped down around them and his cock jumped, wanting its own attention.

Her moans grew deeper and louder. Her cream coated his fingers as he worked them in and out of her core. Allowing her to get close, he never let her go over. Not for a while. As the muscles tightened around him, he leaned closer still and sucked hard on her clit.

Eva bucked hard as she came, his name tearing from her lips.

He fucked her with his fingers until she stopped coming around him, then he withdrew them and seconds later, after covering himself with a condom, pushed deep inside her velvet heat.

Their drinks could wait.

33

Chapter Three

"That's my family."

Grant had her phone and currently sat there looking at the pictures of the Monroe family. "Don't take this the wrong way, but your sisters don't look like you."

She glanced at the image. "Well, Tara loves pink, ergo it's in her hair, and Shai loves purple. So that's why she has a streak of that in hers. I'm the fan favorite of blue."

Eva did her best to ignore the sharp spike of pain upon the knowledge that she wouldn't be able to do this with a child of her own. No pictures, no dying hair. Fucking cancer. Motherfucking, life-sucking cancer.

She would be adopting and that was fine. She loved her sisters more than anything. But she had hoped to be able to have a child of her own, to experience that blessing of carrying a child within her womb. It bothered her that some may not understand this, but it didn't mean she looked any less upon being able to adopt. She wanted to adopt a child or two, but she'd always longed to give birth to one of her own.

"Not what I meant but, yes, I do see the color in their hair."

She narrowed her eyes, anger not far away at any time, but especially when it came to family. "They're my sisters." Her tone was lined with a dangerous warning.

"I don't mean any disrespect, Eva. Far from it, I'm just curious about you and how your family got to be how it is now."

She took a calming breath. Protecting her family was of the utmost importance to her and she would fight anyone who dared be stupid enough to disrespect them. "Sorry, a bit overprotective."

"Figured that."

She rested her chin on his shoulder and gazed at the phone he held. "I'm the biological child and they adopted Tara when she was two. Then they brought in Shai at six months."

"They're beautiful women."

Eva smiled. "Yes, they are. My sisters are gorgeous."

"Don't sell yourself short, babe, you're not too shabby from where I'm standing." He shrugged, bringing her out from behind him. "Or rather sitting."

Eva glared, her anger and tension melting away.

He laughed. "You are absolutely stunning."

"Thanks." She skimmed her finger along the screen, bringing up another picture.

Grant laughed at the image. "What is this one from?"

"This was the night Tara was promoted to ADA."

He gave a low whistle. "She's an assistant district attorney?"

"Yes, don't let her size fool you. She may be shorter than my ass, but she's kickass in the courtroom."

"Hard to tell with the dead piñata on her head." He pointed to the bright blues, purples, reds, greens and yellows that had made up the monster-shaped piñata.

"All part of her deception." She flipped through some others until she found what she sought. "This was taken when Shai got tenure."

"Damn, I'm impressed."

"You should be. We're kickass sisters." She loved them so much and was very proud.

He pointed at the picture. "I'm also going to guess the sparkly green buggy-eyed alien thing on her head isn't an everyday look for her."

"No, not common, unless she's partying. Hell, for all I know, she's wearing that now and nothing else. She's got a wild streak in her when she's not in the classroom."

He turned his head and kissed her cheek. "I'm seeing that." He moved another image. "What's this one?"

"Those are some of my kids."

He pulled back slightly. "Your kids?"

It helped ease the pain of not having any of her own to have these as hers. She loved them and they loved her. "Yes. I'm a pediatric oncologist. These are some of my kids."

Another low whistle left him. "Your parents must be so proud of all of you."

"We like to think so. That's my family. What about you? I mean, I've fucked you repeatedly and I don't even know what you do for a living." She released her phone, leaving it in his hand.

"I'm a surgeon. An ER surgeon. Right now, I'm in Arizona filling in. I was in the Army for a while and was a surgeon there but after a few tours overseas, I got out. I'm part of Doctors Without Borders and so I do a lot of traveling to other countries, just not in the capacity of being a soldier."

Wow. So not like he needs anything else to be damn near perfect. "Any pictures of you on your phone?"

"I've got a few." He dug for his cell and set hers to the side.

The first was one of him in Army camouflage with two other men, all with smiles on their faces.

"That's a great shot," she commented.

"It was a wonderful day."

Something in his tone alerted her that this three-man friendship hadn't all come home. "I'm sorry," she said softly. *Hard for me to convey just how much so.*

"It was war. Not supposed to be glamorous, no matter how much they try to make it seem so in movies and on television. Thanks, though." He cleared his throat and brought up an image of an older couple. "My parents, Howard and Danielle Harrison."

"And what do they do?"

"Retired and traveling the world. Right now, I believe they're over in Italy visiting some friends. I don't know which country they're in. I'm sure wherever they are at they are having a blast."

"Nice." She hugged him. Loving having the ability to touch his body. "I know you mentioned a sibling, but not ever how many you have. So big family? Small?"

"One sister who is also a trauma surgeon. Her name is Lucy."

"Impressive." She rolled to the side, keeping him in her sights, even though she wasn't over his shoulder anymore. "And did you always want to be a surgeon?"

He pursed his lips. "I think so. It's all I can remember wanting to do. Except for one year, Halloween, I went as a cop."

She tried to picture him in a cop uniform but it was honestly so much easier to envision him in scrubs with a white coat draped over his shoulders. She pointed at her chest. "I always went as a princess."

He glanced at her. "Always?"

"Yep. My sisters changed it up, but I was bound and determined that if I continually went as a princess, my prince would find me and sweep me off my feet. Spirit me away to his castle in some far-off land."

"Still going as a princess, this year?"

She chuckled. "Hey, I like dressing up as a princess. Don't judge."

Grant held up his large, strong hands, eyes sparkling with humor. "No judgment here. Just curiosity. Do you even include a tiara?"

She gasped indignant. "Of course I do."

"That, I'd love to see."

"Swing by the Quad Cities at Halloween and come to the hospital party. I'm always there. This year, I'm wearing blue."

"I assumed you would be. You mean there were years of other colors?"

Eva smacked him playfully. "Yes, thank you very much. Before I locked in on blue I wore other colors. I've worn many different ones."

"Sure, you have," he drawled. "So you're like Cinderella on this night?"

"A very naughty Cinderella." She sucked her finger into her mouth. "Very naughty."

"What the hell kind of party is this?"

The gravely tone went from his mouth straight to her clit. Eva laughed until her sides hurt. "Sorry, but your expression was priceless. Like I was going there in some naughty dress. So hopeful."

"Woman," he rumbled. "You can't blame me for hoping."

"It's a children's hospital. Of course, I'm a proper princess."

"And behind closed doors?"

"I can't divulge that information. You'd have to come by and find out firsthand yourself." The moment the words left her mouth, she realized they were an invitation to something much more than this week here in Mexico. She wanted it but at the same time, Eva wanted to snatch them back and put up rows of impenetrable walls.

"I may just do that."

While his words pumped a world of hope into her, she pushed it away. This was just a fling. A time to have fun and get enough sex to last her for a while since when she got back, it would be all about work. So, she let it go, not commenting on his statement. Besides, what man would want an incomplete woman?

The anger inside began to churn once more.

I need to not focus on that right now. I'm here to enjoy this time with him. Not pine about a future I'm not going to have with this man.

"Care to take me dancing tonight?" she asked, lying on her back, fingers lingering along his forearm.

"Absolutely. Where?"

"We can ask at the front desk. I'm sure they have some places they'd recommend."

He gathered her close and nuzzled her neck, sending all kinds of warm fuzzy feelings through her. "Consider it a date."

"Good, because it's been a while since I've shaken my ass on the floor."

He nipped her neck. "Not true. You were shaking your ass on the floor earlier today when I was behind you." Grant smoothed a hand over her ass. "Beautiful image to me, it was."

"Can't have that out in public." She tugged on his shirt. "Perhaps we should get it out of the way, so it's not in your system when we go dancing."

"I'm all for doing it again but I promise you, if I see you shaking this on the floor I'm still going to want to fuck you. Hard."

Eva could say, in all honesty, she felt the same way. "That's then, this is now. Let's see what we can do about it. Shirt off."

He listened with a low growl of approval when she stripped off her top.

She got to her feet and put her hands up in the air, grinding her hips. "Come dance with me."

"My pleasure, Eva." Grant got to his feet.

Soon, nothing else mattered but him, his touch and what he was doing to her.

* * * *

Grant stared down at the petite blonde in his arms. They lay out in a hammock, wrapped together, limbs entwined tight together. She slept and he smiled, thinking she had every right to.

I sure kept her up late last night. Not that it was a one-way thing, for she sure as hell kept him up. Goddamn they were good together.

And they had been up until the warm sun began to rise, bathing the land in its glow. They'd stayed awake long enough to get some breakfast however, she'd wanted to be outside for a bit.

So they climbed into a double hammock at the hotel and had been there ever since. He had two more days here and didn't want to leave her. Hell, he wanted to take her home with him to Arizona and see where things went between them.

"I'm not any good at long-distance relationships. But I'm willing to give it a try for you," he whispered.

She didn't respond, remaining sound asleep.

He rubbed his hands along her back, not denying the thrill running through directly to his cock when she moaned slightly and pressed against him further. He loved how she wanted to be held. And not just a little bit. She wanted to be locked in his embrace to the point where he worried he would be crushing her. Sometimes he swore she was trying to climb into his skin.

"Makes me feel wanted," she'd said one time when he asked twice if she was okay with how hard he held her.

He sure as hell wanted her. In every way possible. And ninety-five percent of the time, he believed she was on the same page with him, but every once in a while, something would flash over her expression and he would hesitate and wonder. Wonder what she was hiding and keeping from him. What secret made her look angry and sad?

Wonder what she'd say if I asked her to marry me? Grant gave a light chuckle then closed his eyes again, body still exhausted. His mind, however, continued to race about the possibilities between them when they returned to the States.

She shifted against him once more and he bit back his groan. Eva had tucked her hands between them and when she moved, she brushed along the edge of his cock. The blood in his body streaked there and pumped him full of steel and lead. There would be no doubting the erection he'd be sporting when they got out of the hammock.

He heard footsteps approaching and opened his eyes in time to see a member of the staff approaching.

The guy flicked his glance between the two of them, smiled and took the empty glasses away, leaving them alone without a word.

Grant liked that about this place. The staff wasn't intrusive. They weren't constantly asking and interrupting if they could get you something. However, if you needed or wanted anything, they weren't hard to find at all.

Right hotel for me to pick.

Doubly so, because of the woman in his arms.

The wind blew warm around them and he could smell the ocean with each breath he took. It wasn't all he could smell. Eva's shampoo, with the scent of fresh, crisp pears also floated to his nose.

She rubbed against him once more and this time the groan fell from his lips. Eva shifted and he glanced down to find her peering up at him, all sexy and rumpled.

"Hey," she muttered.

"Hey yourself, beautiful."

"How long have you been awake?" She rolled her shoulders and snuggled back up to him, something he greatly approved of.

"Not long. One of the staff came by and collected our glasses, I woke up then." Okay, so he'd been awake prior but not long, so it didn't really count in his mind. "Get enough sleep? We could go back to the room and sleep some more."

"You never fell asleep hard, did you? This is my fault because I wanted to be outside. You stayed partially awake to keep an eye on things."

He shrugged. It was the truth.

"How about this? We go back to my room. Utilize the bed, then nap again. Wake up and do some surfing and get something to eat later on."

Grant slid his hand down to cup her ass. "Utilize the bed. Is that an indecent proposal I'm hearing from you, Ms. Monroe?"

Her blue eyes twinkled. "God, I hope it wasn't a decent one."

He squeezed her ass cheek after which he smacked her lightly. "Good, because I really want you on your knees in front of me as I fuck that luscious mouth of yours. Been dreaming about that, and now I've got this hard cock that isn't going to be hidden as we walk across the hotel."

She moved her hand along his length with subtle motions. "Want me to take care of it now? Right here?"

Lord help him, that was one hell of a tempting offer. "Are you telling me you'd jack me off right here, if I wanted it?" Christ, his voice just dropped a few octaves.

"Jack you, suck you, either or. I'm open for options. I mean the hotel may not approve and we probably shouldn't give young kids anything in the realm of education in the sexual variety but yes, if that's what you want, then I will. I'm not coming back here again, I don't know these people."

His dick pushed hard into her hand. What he wouldn't give to have her warm skin on him instead of with a layer of material between them. "Don't tempt me," he warned in a low tone.

She shrugged with a teasing smile. "Okay. No more tempting. I'll be good." She waggled her eyebrows. "For now."

Somehow, he doubted that. His cell phone rang and he mumbled as he reached for it in his pocket, having to shift away from Eva in order to accomplish his feat.

This time, she didn't settle back against him but climbed out of the hammock.

"Where are you going?"

She stretched, arms over her head, drawing her tank tight over her high rounded breasts. "To my room. You take your call. I'll be up there...showering." She gave him a pure sex kitten grin. "You know, soapy water, steam, flushed skin, that kind of thing." After blowing him a kiss, she walked off — leaving him alone in the hammock with an erection that could have drilled for oil.

Frustrated, he swiped his phone and answered, "What?"

"Did I catch you at a bad time, man?"

His best friend, Daniel Erickson, who was also a colleague at the same hospital. Scrubbing a hand over his face, Grant sat up, allowing his feet to dangle over the edge. "Yes."

"What? About to get some pussy from a willing hottie?"

"Something like that. I'm sure you didn't call to ask about the sex I'm having. What's up?"

"I've got your caseload at work, like you know, but I had a question about one of your patients."

Grant immediately shifted into professional mode, pushing away all thoughts of Eva and her naked body soaping up in the shower, her hands gliding over her peach toned skin. *Yeah, push all those thoughts away.* "Which one?"

"He came in the day before you left, Mr. Hancocci."

Skimming his mental banks, he recalled the patient. "Right, Mr. Hancocci, arrived at the ER with the metal pipe embedded in his chest that had occurred during an explosion at his place of employment."

"Yes, him. Was there anything else about him that you can remember? His pressure refuses to come up and it's like he's still bleeding, but we've checked, and you got him sewn up completely. Nice work by the way."

Grant climbed out of the hammock and headed for the lobby. "Nope, I don't recall anything else on him. It was a hellish night. We had a lot of business unfortunately, during my shift. If I had, there would be notes on his sheet. I'm assuming by the call that there wasn't anything there."

"No, just wondered if maybe since you were so busy, you'd thought of something after the fact."

"Damn it. Nope, sorry. I just remember the lead pipe in his chest and the time it took to get him stable."

"All right. Sorry to bother you on vacation. I'll let you go. See you when you get back. And if you'd care to bring me a sweet hottie, I'd greatly appreciate it."

"Not sure how Sarah would feel about that, and while you may be okay in challenging that, she scares the fuck out of me. She'd make my bones dissolve and not leave a trace, so I'm staying away from anything she may view as inappropriate when it comes to you."

"More the merrier," Daniel teased.

He grinned as he stretched. "Sarah isn't even around, is she? You sure as hell don't have the stones to talk that way if she was."

Male laughter filled the line. "Fuck no, she's at work already."

"I'm out. See you in a few days."

"Hey, Grant?"

"Yeah?"

"Have some fun, will you? Don't think of it as a question but more an order."

"I've got a woman waiting in the shower for me. As soon as I get you off the phone, I am going to have lots of fun."

"Well, hell, why didn't you say so? Bye." Daniel hung up with another laugh.

Staring at his phone, Grant shook his head. *He's got my back for sure.* He shoved the phone in his pocket and jogged to the elevator. As it went to Eva's floor, his cock hardened once more, aware of what was there behind the closed door to her room. Personally, he couldn't wait to sink his dick between her thighs and feel that tight heat surrounding him.

Chapter Four

"Tell me, Grant, what's the most amazing place you've gone to with the organization you work with?" Eva lay on the couch, legs over the arm and her head in Grant's lap. She'd hit that fuck-until-you-can't-move line. The man was insatiable, which she wasn't complaining about. However, she had no energy to move. Not at all. Even her dangling legs were still, no slight swinging back and forth, they just hung there.

They'd been talking about what got them into the medical field. Correction, she'd been asking him, believing it was better for him to talk. Kind of a downer for her to say 'I am a cancer survivor, so that's why I wanted to be a doctor.' She wasn't into getting sympathy from him. This wasn't anything more than an upbeat vacation for her.

Her muscles screamed if she tried to shift, but she floated on a cloud of euphoric bliss. This man had taken her to places she'd only read about in romance novels before. The types of stories she had on her Kindle, so no one would know that she was reading them. She tried to avoid the need to justify what she read. Just because she was a surgeon didn't mean she couldn't enjoy being lost in a tale of lust and adventure. So it was easier having them where people couldn't see the covers of the stories.

"I loved Africa. Don't get me wrong, the rest of the world has beauty that's amazing in its own right, but to me, it was Africa. The places in Africa I went to surpassed everything else. I love that continent." He dragged his fingers up and down her bare arm. His voice stroked along her skin, setting it alive once more.

"Have you been to each country?"

"No. I've traveled to a good number of them, but, no, I've yet to reach every country."

"But it's something you would love to do?"

"Absolutely. I love traveling. The people you meet, the cultures. I love all of it. Helping them while I'm there is a bonus." He shifted his fingers so they stroked along her cheek. "What about you? Do you do any traveling?"

"Nope. This is the first vacation I've had in years. I stick close to home. I'd love to travel, but can't ever seem to find the time." *That and my parents don't like me going that far away.*

"Life is short, beautiful. You working where you do, you should know that. Take the adventure when you can. Live your life to the max. Before you know it, you'll be bogged down with children and can't get away to have some 'you time'."

The knife ripping through her chest and into her heart brought tears to her eyes as she tried her best to ensure the pain didn't leech into her reply. "I've heard that before. I don't know. I guess since I know how little time some can have, and I possess the ability to help some children get a few more months with their family, I don't feel right leaving to indulge myself."

"Your parents raised you to take care of others first. An admirable trait, but you deserve to rest and relax. Like now."

She smiled up at him, falling deeper with each moment they spent together. What wasn't to love? He helped people, caring, hot as all get out and a doctor. All the way around, that was a win-win for her. "I didn't do much resting on this trip. I will say, however, that right now, I'm very relaxed. Of course, that could be because I have zero energy to move."

"Just how I like my women." He winked.

'Women', he had jokes. Her sisters would like him. She'd love to introduce them.

"What are you thinking about? You have a small private smile on your face."

Wriggling her toes, she stared at the pink polish. "Just that my sisters would like you. And I wish you could meet them."

"They sound like a lot of fun. I'd love to meet them." He skimmed along her lower lip with his thumb. "Your parents, too."

Those three words slowed her heart as she struggled to maintain an easy breathing pattern. She stared up at him. He wasn't shying away from making eye contact — he was there. Straightforward. "My parents?"

"Seems logical if I started dating their daughter. I'd want to meet the one my child was dating."

"Dating?"

He held her gaze. "I know this was supposed to be a vacation fling, Eva. I get that. I knew that the second we headed for my room after meeting on the beach. But I don't want it to end there. I want more. I want to be with you. Date you. Be able to call you my girlfriend."

She touched his arm, stopping his movements along her skin. "Are you sure, because you look like you swallowed something foul?" As it was, she had to school her own expression, so it didn't do the same thing. She would love to be his girlfriend, but later, would be the pain when he found out she couldn't have children and left her.

His expression smoothed. "I'm positive. I just didn't mean to blurt it out like that. I'd planned on taking you to a nice dinner first."

Ignoring her body's fervent protest, she rolled to her feet then straddled his lap, avoiding the need to rock on his length as it pushed against her core. Perhaps a fuck would get his mind off the thought of a relationship. *But then, perhaps I can just keep it physical and enjoy what he's offering, yet not make it serious.* "It has kind of surpassed a one-night stand hasn't it?"

"I'd like to think so." He curved a hand around the nape of her neck. "And I'd like it continue the way it's heading."

Butterflies fluttered in her gut. What would Tara and Shai think? *That I was considering having a relationship with someone who was supposed to be a week fuck? Will I have the ability to keep it so I don't fall and end up getting hurt?* "Arizona and Iowa aren't exactly neighbors, you know."

He quirked a brow. "I'm aware of the geography. That's minor. We can work logistics out for that. We have phones and can both travel."

She sank her fingers into the hair along the nape of his neck. "That's the other thing. You're off a lot traveling the world helping people. What if there is a hot doctor where you go? Or nurse?"

Find reasons to keep it just fun and not serious. I have to keep myself safe from being hurt.

"Then they stay hot outside of my tent or room. I won't stray, Eva. That's not the type of man I am. I've been surrounded by women in skimpy bikinis since I arrived and none of them mattered to me until you walked into my line of sight. Only one woman here had the power to kick my libido into high gear. You."

She dragged her tongue along her lower lip. *He's not making this easy.* One of the main differences between him and previous men she'd been with, if they'd tried something like that, she wouldn't have believed them for a second, but the words when they came off his lips, she fell for. Hook, line and sinker. He made her long to trust him. To believe what he said.

"I would be committed to our relationship. May need a lot of phone sex or video chat but I wouldn't cheat."

His sincerity floored her. A lot of the men she knew and casually dated wouldn't have been so candid with her. Well, perhaps about the phone sex bit, but not what he wanted. "Phone sex and video chat, huh?"

"What am I supposed to say? But, yes, I want to hear your sexy voice on the phone, whispering naughty things in my ear as I jack off. Or watch you as you play with my pussy." He slid two fingers up the leg of her shorts and grazed along her slit. "Pushing your fingers in and out, begging for my cock, wishing I was with there with you to lap your cream and fuck you. Have you on my face so I can eat your pussy while you are deep throating my cock."

Eva gulped and rocked against his stiffening dick as well as his fingers teasing her clit with featherlike flicks.

I wish I wasn't wearing any clothing. And he called it 'his' pussy.

This man had turned her into a nymphomaniac. A label she'd wear proudly from this day forward. *However, I believe this affliction will only be when it involves this man.*

"Oh, God," she whimpered. "I think that's something we could arrange."

"So, is that a yes?"

She gyrated her hips, bringing his fingers harder on her nub. "Yes." The moan fell from her lips as she allowed her head to drop back. God, he was going to kill her. But she'd go with a huge ass smile on her face.

Grant tightened his grip and drew her face closer to his until they were nose to nose. "You and I will find a way to make this work, Eva Monroe."

Damn, she loved the way her name rolled off his tongue. If he were the devil, she'd buy whatever he wanted to sell or give up anything he asked just to hear it again. And she told him such.

His chuckle wasn't any less decadent. "So if I told you to get out of these clothes?"

"They'd be gone in a second." She panted, still using his fingers as she wished but craving the cock that remained hidden behind a barrier of clothing.

"Good." He finally pushed a finger deep inside her and kissed her as her moan escaped.

Their tongues twined around each other, stroking, sliding, rolling. In and out his fingers moved as she came around it. As the shocks ran through her, he added another and moved them faster.

He broke the kiss and took a quick bite to her lower lip and gave her a wicked grin. "Not now."

She almost pouted. Instead, she recalled her stating she wanted to know more about him.

"You have another two hours of no sex. You have any more questions?" Grant tapped her on the end of her nose.

She released his hair and climbed off his lap, ready to jump him once more the moment he sucked his fingers in his mouth, cleaning off her cream. Keeping it all on the sex would be difficult because she truly did like him and wanted to know more about what made him tick.

"Tell me about what it's like being part of that organization. I mean do you live in huts while you're out there? Tents? Or nice hotels?" Eva stood and shimmed out of her shorts and panties.

Grant's focus lasered in on her in seconds and a low growl emerged from his throat. "What are you doing?" he croaked.

She stared at the tent in his own shorts. "Asking you questions." She pulled off her shirt and let it fall to the floor, leaving her completely naked. "And waiting for an answer." With a smile, she smoothed her hands down her body before she walked to stand between his legs. Bending at the waist, she took hold of his shorts band and tugged. "Lift up."

He did with a grunt and she pulled. Grant's thick erection popped free and she ignored it for a second — not easy to do — to drag the shorts off the rest of the way. "I'm waiting for an answer."

"To what?"

"My question. Where do you stay when you're in these other countries? We don't call them third world anymore. So what, underdeveloped? Isn't that the correct term?"

He cleared his throat a few times. "Yes. And usually, I'm staying in huts or tents. No nice hotels where we are. We go where people need the most help, and that's typically not in an area where there are nice hotels."

"Running water?" She gestured at him. "Shirt off."

He complied, and when he was as naked as she, she climbed back on his lap, aligning his cock against her wetness.

"What?" His question was low and rough, sounding as if he'd gargled with a bucket of gravel.

She rotated her hips. "Just asking if there was running water?"

"Not always, no." His breathing had changed.

"Okay, let's finish out this two-hour-question-and-answer period I still have." She pressed close, her breasts mashing against his chest. "This is going to be fun. No sex, remember?"

"You're going to pay for this torture, Eva," he warned.

"I'm looking forward to that." She nipped his shoulder and rubbed her slit along his length once more. "More than you could possibly imagine."

* * * *

Grant pulled away from Eva's mouth. He didn't want to let her go to get on his plane. She'd accompanied him to the airport, herself having another two days here. "I could extend my stay."

"You have patients waiting for you, Grant. Go on, get on the plane."

"I'm going to miss you, Eva Monroe."

"Likewise." She hugged him tightly as if she loathed to let him go.

He would be fine with that, not keen on leaving her here as it was.

"We have numbers and you'll call when you land, so go. Thank you, for making this the perfect vacation for me." She cupped his cheek.

Resting his forehead against hers, he inhaled deeply, allowing her scent to wash over him once more. Dammit, it was on the tip of his tongue to tell her he'd gone and done something stupid like fall in love with her. He wasn't a boy who played games. He was a man who knew what or who he wanted. And now that he'd found her, he didn't want to let her go.

They shared one more kiss, then he lifted his bag and walked inside the airport. Turning back, she waved with a smile and climbed in the taxi before it pulled away from the curb. He continued on to his flight.

As he settled in to his seat, he sent her a text telling her he was about to take off. Her responding text came within seconds.

Have a safe flight.

Call you when I land.

Her smiley face had his lips turning up a tiny bit. He turned off his phone as they backed away from the gate and stored it as they taxied. The moment they hit cruising altitude, he closed his eyes and tried to sleep.

Dozing was the best he'd accomplished by the time the plane landed in Phoenix. He walked off the plane and dug for his phone. As he waited at baggage claim, he didn't call his sister but instead called Eva.

She didn't pick up and his heart sank. Had she found someone else?

Christ, now I'm whining like a little bitch.

Moments later, his phone vibrated. He looked at it and smiled.

Sorry, on call with my sister. Will call you back when I'm done? Hope you had a good flight.

He smiled until he glanced around, wondering if people were watching him and thinking he was grinning like an idiot. Then decided he didn't give a damn.

Looking forward to it.

Grabbing his bag from the conveyor belt, he strode for the exit and the parking garage. He slid his phone in his pocket and picked up his pace, wanting to be away from the crowds when she called him back. At his vehicle, he unlocked the hatch and tossed in his suitcase. Slipping behind the wheel, he plugged in his phone after he started the engine.

He yanked the parking stub from the visor and shifted into gear to get to the cashier. After paying for his stay, he headed out of Phoenix to his apartment in Glendale. He was tired and wanted nothing more than a shower and some uninterrupted sleep.

Still nothing from Eva, so he dropped his bag by the foot of his bed, stripped from his traveling clothes and walked naked to his bathroom. Reaching in to turn on the water, he put the dirty clothes in his hamper. He put his phone on the bathroom counter, then stepped into the hot stream and groaned.

His muscles were cramped from the flight. He didn't fly first class because he was cheap and tended to save his money to splurge on things when he was overseas. The water pelted his shoulders and he stood there for a moment, enjoying the massage. He washed with his Irish Spring body wash and closed his eyes as he thought of the showers he'd shared with Eva over the past couple of days. His dick stiffened at the thought of her creamy skin lathered with suds.

He ran his hands over his chest, wishing they were hers. Her softer touch that could be firm around his dick as she stroked him.

Squeezing his eyes shut, he held his shaft, pinched the head and took a deep breath. Up and down, he fisted himself, the soap making the gliding motion smooth and slick.

Slick like Eva when she's aroused. Not as hot or tight as her, though, even if he gripped harder. He jerked faster, widening his stance, imagining her kneeling between them, blue eyes up on his face as she sucked him into her mouth.

"Fuck," he uttered.

The swaying of her breasts as she rode him or he fucked her from behind, holding those globes in his hands, pinching and twisting her nipples. The way her pussy sucked him in and didn't want to let him go. All of it ran on a loop in his mind's eye as he jerked off in the rising steam.

He rested his arm on the tile wall of the shower and breathed heavily as he pulled faster. His balls drew tight and he hissed in a breath. Grant came with a low roar as his release shot free.

It wasn't what he craved, but it would do for now. At least until he got his hands on Eva and had her with him.

Finishing up his shower, he stepped out onto the thick mat and reached for a towel. He'd finished tying it around his waist when his cell began to ring. Heart skipping a few beats, he grabbed for it with a smile on his face. One that fell when he saw his sister was calling.

Not that he didn't want to talk to her, but most, he wanted Eva's voice in his ear.

"What's up, sis?"

"Dad had an accident and is in the hospital. I'm booking us flights to Italy. We leave in three hours. Grab a bag and meet me here."

It took his mind a few moments to process what she'd stated. "What happened?"

"Myocardial infarction." A few deep breaths. "It's serious, Grant. He's going to need a CABG. There are also some complications, but Mom couldn't spit it out. She needs us with her right now."

His legs trembled. Shit. The blockage of his arteries was so severe he needed to have a coronary artery bypass graft surgery? He smoothed a hand down his face, wiping off the water dripping down from his hair. "How many vessels?"

"Quadruple."

"How did we not know about this? I know Mom watches what he eats and they exercise, so how the hell did we miss the signs?"

"You know as well as I do that it may not be noticeable." Her voice grew muffled for a moment before getting louder again. "Don't be late, Grant. I have our tickets. Bring your passport."

"I'm on my way."

Dressed in minutes, he dumped his vacation clothing out of his bag and shoved in new. Bag in hand, he scooped up his keys and phone then headed back out the door he'd just come in a short time ago.

He made it to the airport in record time. His sister texted him where to meet her and he parked before rushing in. She stood where she'd said she'd be and he took her in for a moment. She looked small and tiny, the baby sister he used to protect and tease, not the capable woman he knew she was.

This had her rattled to the core.

"Lucy," he said, approaching her.

"Grant, thank God." She ran to him and wrapped her arms around him. "What if—"

"No." He refused to consider that in any regard. "Do not even go there. He's strong. We have to be strong for Mom."

She nodded, released him, and wiped off her cheeks. "Right. Let's go." Digging into her pocket, she pulled out his ticket. "Here you go."

They made their way to security and through that, with an extra pat down, they were on their way to the gate. He pulled out his cell after they reached there and checked to see if he'd missed the call from Eva.

Nothing.

He could go for hearing her voice right about now. Instead of calling, he sent her a text message.

About to board a plane for Italy. Will call you later after I land.

"Who's put the silly grin on your face?" Lucy asked as he sat beside her.

"What?"

"Don't play dumb with me, big brother. I never seen that look on your face before, so I'm assuming it's from a girl. Who is she? What does she do? Where does she live? When do we get to meet her?"

"Slow down there, sis." He shook his head over her grin. At least she wasn't crying, so he could take her ribbing. Besides, he did want them to meet. He didn't have any plans of allowing Eva to run out of his life.

"You met her recently, right? Last time I saw you this glow wasn't there. You were tired. Now you're tired with a glow."

"It's called sweat, sis. We live in Arizona, it's hot."

She shook her head. "We're in air conditioning."

"And I'd just gotten out of the shower when you called."

Another shake. "Try again, brother dearest."

Grant sighed. "I met her on my vacation, all right?"

Her brilliant smile tugged at him. They'd almost lost her in a car accident when she was sixteen. It had taken a long time for her to recover, and walk again, much less be able to stand for the hours required to do a job in the emergency room.

"And?" she drew out. "What's her name?"

"Eva."

"Sounds like a princess. But I'll not judge, yet. What does she do?"

"She's a pediatric oncologist."

"I like her already."

So did he. Grant leaned over and kissed his sister on the cheek. "So do I, sis. So do I." He waited for their plane to board, all the while, checking for a message from Eva.

Chapter Five

Eva scowled as she dashed up the sidewalk to the hospital. She'd tried to call Grant numerous times since receiving his text about going to Italy.

There'd been nothing, no responding text, no calls. Nada. Zip. Zero. The man could have fallen off the face of the earth and she would know the same information she did now.

"Morning, Dr. Monroe."

"Morning, Jeffery," her automatic reply fell as she passed the front desk on her way to the staff's break room.

"How was your vacation?"

"Just what I needed."

"Must have been great with the sex until you no longer move."

She stepped back to face the man at the counter, blinking before she stared at him in shock. It hit her. Amber Eyes. He had been the man in the bar who'd watched her with smiling eyes.

Eva covered her face, knowing it heated with her embarrassment. "I can't believe you heard that. I suppose everyone heard that."

He nodded. "Pretty much. Don't worry about it. Just having some fun."

"Thank you for that at least."

So what if I fell for the man I was just supposed to have a fling with? So what, if he hasn't called me back or texted me? I'm a big girl, I can handle the disappointment. Wasn't supposed to be attached to him anyway.

The man, bless his heart, didn't know she was pining for someone, so he just smiled and congratulated her once more on a great vacation.

She continued on to the staff room and pushed into the darkened interior.

"I'm fucking miserable," she groused as she opened her locker and pulled out her scrubs.

She would give herself until she changed and walked back out to sulk and feel sorry for herself. Then she had to have her game face on and be happy. These small children were in the fight of their lives and she, with her minor man issues, wasn't at all important or worth crying over.

"Get over yourself, Eva," she said to her reflection in her locker mirror. Reaching back in, she pulled out a coral reef skull cap and put it on her head. She made a point to wear something bright and cheerful. So the colorful fish would be great for the day.

With one final pep talk, she headed for the door to begin her day. It was a busy one and she didn't have time to think about the man she'd met in Mexico. There were children to focus on and save.

Her nurse, Michela, met her at the door, clipboard in hand.

"Morning, Michela."

"Doc," she greeted with a smile, white teeth sticking out against her darker skin, courtesy of her Latin heritage. "Surgery in twenty minutes. Here's the chart on Jacob. They're prepping him now."

"Thanks." Eva took the offered chart and read over the stats of the five-year-old she was about to put under her knife. They were operating to remove a tumorous mass on his lung. This was the child's third surgery in his young life and the first she'd done for him. "I want his most recent X-rays up, so I can take a look at them. Where are his parents?"

"Last I saw, they were in the chapel."

"I'll go talk to them, then I'll be in. Make sure those films are there."

"Yes, ma'am."

Eva handed back the chart and strode off in the opposite direction Michela headed. She checked her watch, pushed into the chapel and looked around the quiet room.

On the left side, a couple sat, holding hands and praying.

Hands in her scrubs, she walked to the end of the pew and waited for them to notice her.

"Dr. Monroe," the father said.

"Don't get up," she said, holding out her hand. "I just wanted to stop by and talk to you before the surgery. We're prepping your son now. I want you to know, I'm going to do everything I can for him to get this tumor off his lung. The surgery will take a few hours, but I will have a nurse come by with updates for you. I know you're going to worry, you're parents, I just didn't want you to not hear anything during the time we're operating."

"The others didn't do that," Mr. Phillips said, sliding closer to Eva.

"I'm not other surgeons, Mr. Phillips. I can only do what I can do. I understand that this is an extremely scary and stressful time. Please, be assured your son will be looked after as if he were my own."

"I heard you were the one to see. They said you are the best."

She just smiled softly. "I have to go now, but after the surgery is finished, I will come talk to you personally, okay?"

He reached for her hand and squeezed. "Thank you. Please, please help our boy."

"I will do everything in my power to do just that. I'll talk to you in a few hours." She rose and left them alone in the chapel.

As she scrubbed, she looked in the room, pleased to see her team there, ready for her. Jacob lay there, being monitored. She backed in, arms up and was gowned and gloved right away.

Then she stopped to study the films hanging, just to make sure her previous thoughts would continue to work. Content everything still looked the same, she turned to the table. "Morning, everyone."

Replies came from behind the masks of her people.

"Music today, Doc?"

She stepped up to the table and took a moment to stare at the small child lying there. "I think today we need something uplifting."

"I have just the music for that," he said.

The first notes piped into the room and she smiled, loving John Dreamer's music as *True Strength* was one of her favorite pieces by him. "Good selection, Ron. Let's get this boy fixed up, shall we?" She reached for the scalpel and leaned over him, taking a breath then making the first incision, the red blood starkly visible against his pale skin.

* * * *

Five consultations and her rounds finished, Eva sat at her desk and groaned, leaning back.

"You okay, Doc?"

"Know what the worst thing about a vacation is, Michela? Coming back to work. I need a vacation from my vacation, just to recover."

The nurse laughed.

Eva slanted her gaze to her. "I'm telling you the truth. I am still exhausted."

"I'm sure you are. It was all that sex you were having."

Her body flushed at the mention of sex. Cripes, she had to get a grip. "Something like that," she hedged.

Michela snorted. "Oh, please. You came back looking all relaxed and sated. You can play it off if you want, but we all know the truth. You had your clock cleaned. Your world rocked. Tires rotated."

She sat forward, hands out. "Please, stop. I get it. You think I had wild, crazy, amazing sex."

Her friend crossed her arms and arched a finely plucked black eyebrow. "Tell me I'm wrong."

She couldn't, not even a little bit.

Michela knew it and laughed harder this time around. "May want to work on that before the others catch up to you. They're going to want all the details."

"And you don't?"

"I plan on having them tonight at dinner. We're still on, right?"

"Yes, I'm not saying no to one of your meals."

"You just love me for my cooking skills."

"At least I'm honest about it." Eva shrugged with as much innocence as she could muster. To tell the truth, it wasn't all that much.

"You've got it bad for him. I can't wait to hear all about it. But not now. We have a party to get to."

This time her smile was wide and full of happiness. Eva pushed to her feet. "Yes, we do."

One of their patients had a birthday today and the staff today was celebrating it with her. There was cake and ice cream for those who could have it and fruit for the ones who couldn't.

Straightening her cap, she beckoned to her friend. "Let's go." She pocketed her phone without looking at the screen. Eva would think about Grant later, once she made it to her apartment.

* * * *

Grant stared off at the wall, seeing nothing. His heart was broken and he didn't know how to fix it.

The house was quiet, his mother and sister finally having fallen asleep. He pushed up from the sofa and paced before the large bay window. Outside clouds rolled in, starting to hide the stars and the moon. The occasional flash of lightning forewarned of an impending storm.

However strong it was, there wouldn't be any way for it to erase the pain flooding him.

He reached for his phone and dialed Eva, not paying attention to the time.

She answered on the second ring. "Dr. Monroe."

"Eva?"

"Who is this?"

He blinked, suddenly understanding, it was three in the morning for her. "I'm sorry, this is Grant. Grant Harrison, from Puerto Vallarta."

He heard her shifting on the bed. "I'm sorry. I didn't recognize your voice. You sound horrible. Is everything okay? I tried calling you a few times but you never got back to me."

Pinching the bridge of his nose, he willed back the tears burning in the corners of his eyes. "I know, and I'm sorry. I was called to Italy when my father had a massive heart attack." Her sharp intake was the only sound she made and he continued, "He didn't make it out of bypass surgery." His voice trembled and he didn't give a damn. "My father is gone. I never even got to tell him goodbye."

"Sweet Jesus. I'm so sorry, Grant. How are your mom and sister? Are you with them now?"

"They finally went to sleep. I gave Mom a sleeping pill and my sister just finally crashed." He moved outside to the patio and sat in the chair his father had used as long as Grant could remember. If he closed his eyes, he could still smell the hint of tobacco from his old man's pipe. "I'm sorry for calling you. I know you probably have — "

"Don't you dare apologize for that. You needed me, I'm here. What can I do?"

"Talk to me. I don't know what I'm supposed to do. I give the message to people all the time when a patient is lost on the table. That is different. It shouldn't be, but it is."

"Of course, it is," she chimed in, her voice soft but lined with steel. "This is your father who is gone. You don't have to be the one who's strong and delivering the news. You're the son. You're allowed to grieve."

"No, I have to be strong for my mom and my sister."

"They're sleeping right now, Grant. This is time for you."

The first of the tears leaked free and he allowed it to fall. His throat hurt and he longed to run out into the desert and scream into the night sky. "Eva." Her name ripped from his throat on a tortured moan.

"Tell me about him. Tell me about your father."

"Are you sure I'm not disturbing you?"

"Grant. Enough. You called me, I'm here for you. Talk to me. This isn't something you can keep bottled up. Or shouldn't."

He stretched out his legs and leaned back in the chair as he began to talk. Earliest memories, things his father had taught him. Memories he'd held dear that would be even more cherished now. When the sun rose, he realized he'd been on the phone with her for four hours and never once had she told him she had to go. Never once had she tried to rush him along.

Eva allowed him to speak and talk, as he wanted. However, once he began, it all flew free from his mouth to her ears. "I'm sorry I kept you up all night."

"I'd do it again in a heartbeat, Grant. Are you feeling any better?"

"A little, thank you, Eva. I should let you go. There are a few final touches we have to put on the funeral that's a day off."

"If you need me, call, Grant. I'll have my phone with me all day. Take care of yourself." She hung up.

He remained in the chair as the door behind him opened, allowing his sister to step up beside him. Lucy sank to the arm of the chair and rested against him.

Together, they sat there as the sun finished cresting the horizon, bringing in a new day to the lovely state of Arizona.

"Did you get any sleep?" she asked.

"No. I'll sleep later. I'm going to go take a shower, grab some breakfast then tend to the last things that have to be done for tomorrow."

"I can help."

"I know you can, Lucy, but I think Mom needs you more right now. Don't worry, I've got it handled."

"You always have it all handled." She kissed his cheek. "I love you, Grant."

"Right back atcha, little sister." He squeezed her leg then rose and went inside.

After eating, he went to his pearl Laredo and slid behind the wheel. He drove from his parents' house to the funeral home to set up final arrangements for tomorrow. Nothing could go wrong or he'd never forgive himself.

On his way back, he called Daniel.

"Hey, man, how are you doing?" Daniel asked immediately.

"I'll be okay, thanks. Just checking in to make sure everything is fine."

"Don't worry, I've got you covered both today and for most of tomorrow. I'll be at the funeral and for the time I'm there, we have Jenna to cover. So don't worry about it. Sarah is also taking the day off and will be around to help Lucy and your mother with anything they may need after."

"Thanks, man."

"He was a father to me, as well, and you're my brother. I wouldn't be anywhere else."

"I appreciate it. Thank you."

"You never have to thank me, man, but you're welcome. Call if there's anything else I can do."

"Will do." He ended the call and pulled into a restaurant that he'd called ahead to have curbside service for, checking his phone. There was one missed text from Eva.

Thinking of you. Just wanted you to know that. No need to call but I'm here if you want to talk some more.

That was it. Nothing else and he saved the message as he climbed from the Jeep. After paying for dinner, he got back in his SUV and headed back home. The closer he got, the tighter the knot in his chest became, breathing grew more difficult, and he pulled over to the side of the road.

Get it together. You have to be strong for Mom and Lucy. He rubbed his scruff, stared at his expression in the rearview and shook his head.

Back on the road, he turned on the radio, trying to drown out the memories that wouldn't let him alone.

His mom sat in her chair knitting when he walked through the door with their food.

"Hi, Mom," he said, bending down to kiss her cheek.

"Hey, baby. You sister is taking a nap, so we can eat when she wakes."

"Can I get you anything now? Tea? Water?"

She shook her head, looking older than he'd ever seen her. In just a few days, she'd gone from youthful and energetic to old and exhausted. "No, thank you, baby. I thought I'd just sit here and knit your father some socks. You know his feet get cold so easily."

Grant nodded and walked away, dropping the food off in the kitchen. *Is she losing it? Does she think Dad is still alive?*

After a moment or two, he went back to the living room and sat on the coffee table, facing her. "Mom," he began. "About what you said, the knitting socks for Dad."

"I know he's gone, baby. It doesn't matter. He will have them with him in the casket. A pair of warm socks."

Tears streamed down her face and he blinked back his own. "Yes, ma'am."

Dinner was a somber affair and he went to bed with a heavy heart. When he woke in the morning, it didn't matter that the clouds were nonexistent and the sky as blue as you could wish for, his heart was black and full of sorrowful pain.

Grant smoothed his hand down his suit coat and left his room. Gathering his mother and sister in his vehicle, he then drove them to the funeral home. They were going to have a final private viewing before the funeral actually started.

As his mother and sister cried by the casket, he walked around looking at all the flowers and plants that had been sent. His father was a well-loved man and it showed. He paused beside a standing spray basket in blue and white. Simple, elegant and beautiful.

He reached for the card and smiled.

The angels in heaven have welcomed home your loved one so he can stand watch over you with a new army. He is never gone, will never be forgotten, and will always love you.

Our sincerest condolences on your loss.

The Monroe Family

Eva. He closed his eyes and took several breaths. Her thoughtfulness touched him.

The director approached him. "We're about to open to everyone, is that okay?"

Replacing the card, he nodded. "Yes, thank you."

With his mom and sister, they began welcoming and thanking people as they entered. Family, friends, the place filled swiftly. As people mingled and said their farewells, as he turned to the door in time to see a town car pull up. Grant moved to greet whomever had arrived and his heart stuttered to a stop.

Eva stepped out from the darkened interior, a black dress hugging her curves. The heels put her higher than her five-three frame. The rounded neckline was modest, giving her attire a timeless look. The three-quarter sleeves made it not overly sexy. Or so he thought until she walked, showing him the slit on the left side. His heart thundered in his ears and he gulped, desperately trying to put moisture back into his mouth.

A simple gold pendant hung around her neck, the cross shone in the sun. In one hand, she carried a black clutch. She thanked the driver then approached him.

"Eva," he said, striding to meet her partway. "What are you doing here?"

"You said you needed me, Grant." She touched his face, fingers sliding along the shadowed growth on his jaw. "So here I am."

Chapter Six

Eva hoped she hadn't overstepped, but the anguish lining his voice had ripped through her, tearing her apart in ways she didn't think could happen for a man she'd just met. But it had. She'd called her sisters and spoken to them about it.

Tara and Shai had both agreed right away for her to fly out to Arizona and be there for the man who'd claimed a part of her heart. They hadn't even paused when she said the guy from her vacation had called her to say his father had passed. Her sisters ruled, and bless them, family came first, and they felt she should be with him. Because they supported her instantaneously, she'd boarded a plane. They sent the flowers, so she didn't have to worry about it and she came to be with Grant, offering whatever support she could.

He leaned into her touch, briefly closing his eyes as if memorizing the feel of her hand against his skin. Grant's eyes still pierced through her when he locked onto hers. She gulped, wanting to lean in close and press to him, allow his arms to close about her, make her feel as if nothing in the world could touch her.

This isn't about me, it's about being there for him during this time, so he can help out with whatever his family needs and be the grieving son.

Turning his head so his lips connected to her palm, he kissed her. "Thank you," he whispered. He took her hand and led her back inside the funeral home. As expected, based on the number of vehicles in the parking lot, there was a big group there to say their farewells.

As they walked into the main room, he laced their fingers together and walked up to a woman who could be none other than his mother. Her eyes were red rimmed from her crying but she dabbed the corners and put on a fake smile.

"Mom, I'd like you to meet my friend Eva."

She released his hand and took his mom's. "I'm so sorry for your loss."

"Thank you for coming. How do you know my son?"

A question she'd been expecting. *I mean, really it was a funeral and there I am showing up, never having met any of the family previously.* "I'm a doctor, as well."

"Oh," she said with a nod. "Thank you again."

She moved away and Eva looked to Grant. "I thought that may be the easiest explanation."

He kissed the top of her hand, his eyes speaking more than words ever could.

She met others in his family, their friends and former colleagues. Eva stayed in the back during the service.

As they began leaving to head for the cemetery, Grant had her beside him once more. "I want you with me."

"Are you sure I should be in the family limo?"

"Yes." His answer fell absolute and instantaneous.

"All right, then." She withstood the looks from his sister and mother during the ride but didn't pay them much mind. Sure, they were watching her and looking at her as if she didn't belong, and perhaps she didn't, but he wanted her there, and so there she'd be.

Eva stood behind him at the service at the site, occasionally touching the back of his neck and shoulders in a silent show of support. She paid her respects then got back in the limo with them and headed to the house.

This was where she got to work. Ensuring people had enough to eat, that drinks remained full, she walked around doing the small tasks, so the family could visit with those who knew him and would miss him so much. She helped out a sweet, small Navajo woman named Sarah who was the wife of another doctor Grant worked with. Sarah was a lovely woman. A few smatterings of quiet laughter broke occasionally and she figured they were remembering better times.

The day passed and she stood in the kitchen, washing dishes by hand from those who'd brought food to the house, making sure they were dry and ready to be taken home. Standing by the sink, she was drying a casserole dish when Grant walked in.

She glanced up at him with a soft smile on her lips. "How are you holding up?" She put down the dry dish and rested the towel on the counter.

"I'd be lying if I said it was easy. What are you doing in here? You don't have to be doing dishes. Go sit down, get something to eat and why are you shaking your head at me?"

Eva stepped flush to the man who towered over her by a good seven inches when she didn't have heels on. Even with them on, she had to tilt her head back to meet his gaze. "I've eaten. Don't worry about me, Grant. Do what you have to out there. I'll be in here doing the small things and making sure people are taken care of food and drink wise."

"You also took the children aside and talked to them. They seem a bit more comfortable with what's going on. How did you do that?"

"I've learned how to deliver news of death to children, Grant. I do that daily at work, I've discovered a way to express it in a way they understand."

A woman in a black dress two sizes too small for her large frame walked in the kitchen. "I'm sorry. I was told my dishes were in here."

"Mrs. Mulroney, yes of course," Eva said, moving back from Grant. "I have them over here for you. Cleaned and in a bag for carrying." Hefting the paper bag, she handed it to the gray-haired woman. "Thank you so much for your dishes, they were delicious."

"Aren't you just a gem? So nice of you to come out and help during this day. I mean, you're so sweet, I hardly notice the blue in your hair."

Releasing the handles, Eva smiled. "Thank you. Drive safely." She returned to drying dishes as Mrs. Mulroney said goodbye to Grant, as well.

Moments later, it was just the two of them in the kitchen again.

Grant pinned her between him and the counter. "How do you do it?"

"Do what?" Lord help her, he smelled so inviting and dangerously decadent.

"You never met the woman, yet you knew the dishes she'd brought with her."

76

"I asked. When I spoke with people, I found out who brought what. Plus, some people arrived with dishes and I just remembered who brought which dish."

Grant settled a calloused hand along her cheek. "I want to kiss you so damn bad."

His admission went directly from his lips to her clit. Pushing up on her toes, she brushed her mouth along his jaw, his stubble teasing her lips. "Go be with your family. I've got this part handled."

When he left, she got back to work, putting clean dishes in bags and leaving them on the table. Then she walked back out and made sure the desserts were still doing fine, refilling coffee or getting more tea for people.

After the last person left, she was back in the kitchen, finishing up the dishes. Her feet screamed, but she ignored their cries. Not much longer and she would be out of these shoes.

"You can stop now," Grant said from behind her.

"Food's all labeled and put away in the fridge. Some people forgot to take their dishes, but each bag is labeled, so you or your sister can return them without guessing who belongs to what. This is the last of the dishes to wash, so I'll be out of your hair in a few minutes."

He closed his arms around her waist and buried his face along her neck. "I don't want you to leave."

"I'm not sleeping here, Grant. I have a room at the Hilton nearby. I'll grab a cab and head over."

"No." His hard body pressed against hers.

Eva could feel his dick pushing into the small of her back. "No?"

"I'll take you. You've done so much, I'll be damned if I let you go back in a cab."

"I'll be ready in a few minutes."

He kissed her neck and she bit back her whimper. Christ, all she'd thought about since leaving him in Mexico was his touch, his kisses, how he set her body aflame. Not true, she'd missed just being with him, something about him made her relax and want to stop and enjoy life.

Stop thinking like this, Eva. Now isn't the time.

She finished up the dishes and walked back through the large house to the living room where he waited with his mother and sister.

They both looked at her and rose. Eva got hugs from both women and kisses on the cheek.

"Thank you," his sister said. "For everything. And for being here for my brother. I see why he loves you."

Eva didn't know what to say to that, but it didn't matter. His mother hugged her next with a gratitude of her own.

Grant took her hand and led her out to where a black BMW waited, running with its parking lights on. He held the door for her and assisted her inside.

She groaned as she sat, having been on her feet all day not the issue, the problem was she'd been in heels all damn day and that was a new thing for her. At the hospital, she wasn't in heels this high. Hell, most days she wore tennis shoes or Crocs. These types of shoes were reserved for nights out with her sisters or the few and far between dates that she hadn't had in forever.

"Downtown?"

"Yes."

They rode in silence, but he captured her hand and interlace their fingers once more. He pulled up to the hotel and instead of stopping in front of the door, and letting her out, he gave the car over to the waiting valet and came around to help her.

Taking his hand as he opened the door, she glanced over at him. "You could have just dropped me off."

"I'm walking you up."

She wouldn't argue. Side by side, they walked in the hotel and headed for the elevator.

At the door, he took her key from her and opened it.

Silence fell between them as they entered.

Eva took off her shoes and groaned as her feet hit flat on the floor.

"You okay?" he asked, moving to her side.

"I'm not used to being on my feet all day in heels that high. I don't wear those types of shoes to the hospital." She ran a hand through her hair. "Thank you for walking me up. I'm here, I'm fine. Go be with your family. I can't believe you gave your car to the valet just to escort me up here." Her belly clenched as he ran his tongue along his lips. God, she wanted him so badly, but she wasn't going to initiate anything. If he did, she sure as hell wouldn't say no, but she wasn't making the first move.

Grant shrugged out of his suit coat and draped it over the nearest chair to him. His tie followed, and damn was it sexy to watch a man remove a tie. Then he unbuttoned his shirt, exposing his golden skin as the crisp white cotton fell away.

She resisted the urge to squeeze her legs together and rock.

He rolled his shoulders and the shirt fell down his arms before he tossed it to land on his coat. "I still need you, Eva."

That's all she needed to hear. Standing there in the dress, she curled her toes into the carpet beneath her feet and nodded.

"Help me forget."

"Stop," she ordered when he put his hands on the fastener for his pants. She moved closer and brushed his away. "Allow me."

* * * *

Grant exhaled slowly as Eva stood there unbuttoning his pants. God, he'd missed her touch something fierce. The backs of her fingers brushed against his gut and his cock swelled further. He'd been semi-aroused all damn day because of her nearness.

The way the black dress curved about her body, leaving nothing to his imagination and fueling the fire he had for her with its simple elegance and sexiness. This woman was hot as sin and he accepted she could burn him without even trying.

The zipper was the only sound in the hotel room as she drew the tab down. She brushed back the open flaps and reached back to slip her hand inside his boxers.

This time, the groan didn't remain in his throat but slid free into the air.

Her warm hand curled around his still thickening member. He bucked his hips slightly and she tightened her hold in response. With her free hand, she pushed down his pants to his ankles then carefully did the same to his boxers.

Grant watched her.

She fixated on his dick in her hand, eyes not wavering as she stared at her hand stroking him. Eva sank to her knees her warm breath dusting along the large head. She opened her mouth and took him in, encasing him with her wet heat.

"Eva," he growled.

She tipped her head to peer up at him with her big blue eyes.

Christ, what a sexy sight. This woman wearing a black dress, no shoes, with blue tips in her blonde hair, on her knees before him, his dick in her mouth, and she watched him.

"I'm not going to put up with this for long," he warned. "I need to be deep inside your pussy."

She released his dick with a pop and pushed back to her feet. Three steps away, she bent over the couch, lifting her dress showing him the black thong she wore. "So come on, then."

It didn't matter his pants were around his damn ankles, he was to her in seconds and had snapped the thong from her body, dropping it beside them. Nudging her legs wider, he pushed balls-deep inside her with a single stroke. She'd been turned on by sucking him for her slit was wet as it welcomed him. "Shit," he moaned.

A comment echoed by the woman beneath him.

Grant gripped her hips, one hand on flesh the other gripping the dress bunched up as he began thrusting in and out of her. Each stroke faster, harder, and deeper than the previous, until he couldn't tell where she began and he ended.

Rotating her hips, Eva begged for more with each pound.

His fingers bit into her as he anchored them together as his cock jerked, filling her with his release. Panting hard, he bent over her body as he pried his shoes off his feet and shed the pants along with boxers around his ankles. He lifted her, their bodies still joined, and carried her to the bed.

Laying her on the mattress, he pushed deeper into her—eliciting another moan from her. Using his left hand, he undid the zipper to her dress. Kissing her exposed skin along the way, he took a moment and nipped her shoulder before pulling out of her body. "Get out of that dress."

Eva turned to look at him, wriggled her shoulders and the item slid down her body pooling at her feet, leaving her wearing nothing but that chain around her neck. She captured her lower lip with her teeth and beckoned to him.

Grant listened and moved close enough, so their torsos touched.

She wound her arms around him and rested her head over his heart. "You need me, I'm here."

* * * *

He lay her back on the mattress and stood over her, observing her hungrily. Damn, he couldn't get enough of her. He picked up one foot and kissed it before moving up her leg. Then he stopped at the top of her thigh, somehow avoiding her pussy and made the same action for her other leg. He continued on his way up her body, over her belly, briefly tonguing her belly button, and moving on. At her breasts, he teased, flicking his tongue along the pebbled tips.

Her breathing increased and hitched.

As he enjoyed one, he used his hand on the other, and switched until she was squirming beneath him. Then he headed up again, until he reached her mouth.

Capturing it, he tangled with her tongue for a bit, before he rolled them so she was on top of him.

She watched him but didn't speak, just waited.

Grant realized she'd meant what she'd said. She was there for him. Gripping her ass, he rubbed his dick against her core. "Get up here."

Instead of listening as he'd thought she would, she shook her head once and turned around, presenting him with her back. Rising slightly, she then came back down, taking his hardness deep inside her.

Moaning, Grant waited to see what she was going to do next.

She leaned forward, extending her feet back to his shoulders and putting her upper body between his legs. Then she began to move.

Holy fuck.

Eva used his feet to give herself added leverage and pushing power as she slid up and down on his cock.

He stared at her ass as it moved before him and he tried to slow the rush of pleasure coursing through him, drawing his balls up tight, but it was no good.

She was too good.

Holding her hips, he helped increase the speed and friction by pushing her onto him even more. "Christ, Eva," he ground out. "I'm about to come again."

She did, coating his dick with her cream.

He slammed into her once more, then came hard, filling her.

The mattress muffled her cry but he got the gist of the line of swearwords that fell from her lips. As soon as she stopped shaking, she slithered forward off his cock, turned back to him and moved up until she was over him again.

He tugged her down to his chest and wrapped his arms around her. "Where the hell did you learn that?"

"*Kama Sutra.*"

"Jesus." He kissed her forehead.

"You know you should be getting back to check on your mom and sister."

"I want to stay here."

"They may need you around, Grant."

She was right and, with reluctance, he climbed from the bed and padded to the bathroom. When he returned, cleaned up and dressed, she remained lying in the bed. Her clothing still piled on the floor.

"How long are you here for?"

"A few more days."

He strode to the bed and bent to kiss her. "I'll be by for breakfast."

"I'll be here."

Damn, he didn't want to leave her. He wanted to curl up beside her and forget everything for a while. Swiping his suitcoat, he shrugged into it and sighed again. "See you in a while, Eva."

She climbed from the bed and he stared at her until she covered her naked body with a long shirt she pulled from her bag. She walked up to him and wrapped her arms around him. "I'm so sorry for your loss."

"And I'm so grateful you were here." He guided her chin up with one finger and brushed their mouths together ever so brief, knowing if he allowed it to be longer, he wouldn't leave the room. "Sleep well, beautiful."

He left before he stayed all night. Grant cast several glances to the door as he waited for the elevator to come, wishing he could go back in to Eva.

Chapter Seven

"And what happened after the wonderful days of marathon sex? Did you at least set a time to see each other again?"

Eva glared at her sister Tara. "Does everything out of your mouth have to be so damn loud?"

No shame appeared in her sister's expression in the slightest. Her almond-shaped black eyes sparkled in the lights of the restaurant. "Yes, when it comes to sex. I'm a moaner. Actually, more of a screamer. Well, if the man knows what he's doing, that is."

"I swear you do this to me just because you can."

"Of course, I do. What were you thinking?" Tara sipped her drink and gave her a shit-eating grin.

"Good point." She glanced at her watch. "Where's Shai? She's usually the most punctual of us all."

"No clue. Haven't heard from her today. In fact, I've not heard from her for a few days. She's been different since she got back from her trip. Kind of like you have been." She took another drink. "I forgot to ask. How was the funeral?"

"Beautiful as far as funerals go. His family was nice. His father must have been a well-known person and well liked, there were a lot of people there. The arrangement you all sent was beautiful, so thank you for handling that."

"Wonderful, so glad it turned out nice. And how was Grant with you showing up?"

Part of what she loved about her siblings was their ability to change direction in a heartbeat. She didn't want to discuss sex in a restaurant, so her sister asked about something else without much pain.

Her salmon and Tara's shrimp came. "I think he was glad to see me. I didn't spend much time with him at the funeral. I took care of the food, drinks, and cleanup. Also dealt with some of the children who were having a harder time."

Tara nodded. "You are good at that. I expect to see you with a brood of your own soon."

"Really? Now, you're trying to get me to be a mother? I'm busy with my career, not sure when I would be having tons of time to raise a family. Plus, let's not forget that there's not a man there who could contribute to this cause." There were times when she figured her sisters forgot she couldn't have kids and she struggled to ignore the shaft of pain radiating through her.

She stopped and blinked a few times, the fork wobbling in her trembling hand. *I just remembered that we had unprotected sex. Three times. I could be pregnant right now. If not for the cancer, the motherfucking cancer.*

"Everything okay, Eva?"

With a glance to her sister, she spied the other one walking through the crowd of patrons to them. "Fine. Just saw Shai come in."

Tara turned as well.

Shai strode up and smiled at the two of them. "Sorry. Classes ran late."

Eva and Tara shared a look.

"What?" Shai asked. "They did."

"I thought your last class was three hours ago." Tara ate a shrimp.

Shai sat and placed her order for food and drink. She put her purse on the back of her chair. "Mine was, but I stepped in for Professor Harptin and one of his calculus classes." She rubbed her hands together. "What'd I miss? Have we found out about the funeral yet?"

Eva smiled and caught Shai up while they waited for her food.

"And what about the days after the funeral?" Shai questioned. "Did you learn to love Phoenix or have you still not seen much of the city because you didn't leave your hotel room?"

"Seriously? What is it with both of you and the need to know about my sex life?"

"We're nosy and we're your sisters. Why are you shocked?" Tara looked to Shai. "Why is she shocked?"

"Must be something that happens in med school. I mean, it only happened to her, not either one of us." Shai drank her martini and sighed happily. "Some days that's all that's needed."

"Nasty drink," Tara snipped. "You should have some class and drink a chard."

"Thank you. I'd rather drink shards of glass than that crap."

Eva let it go because if they were arguing with each other, they weren't on her about her sex life and how many times she and Grant fucked in her hotel room before she left Arizona and returned to Iowa.

As one, both women stopped and stared at her.

Damn it, it's like they read my mind. Eva kept her expression as blank as possible, but around her sisters, it meant nothing at all.

"I believe you were about to tell us how Arizona was."

"Nope, pretty damn sure I wasn't."

"Cute…how she thinks after so many years that it's actually going to work," Tara said to Shai.

"You know us, we can just get louder if you don't tell us what we want to know."

No idle threat coming from those two.

Eva took a deep breath and filled them in, leaving out some of the more descriptive acts.

"So I have to ask, Eva. How serious is it with you and Grant?"

She bit back her instinctive flippant response. This was Shai who asked and her other sister who also wanted to know. "I like him. A lot. I mean, a lot, a lot."

"And I'm guessing he feels the same way?" Shai ate a hushpuppy.

"I believe so. Christ, you would think after all this time… Hell, I'm a respected and sought-after surgeon. I'm damn good at what I do, but this man—he makes me feel like I'm back in high school, all giggly and stupid."

They didn't laugh at her, in fact, they didn't say a thing, and she flicked her glance between the two of them. "Nothing to say?"

"Nope, not other than what are you going to do about it?"

"I have a question." Tara pointed her fork. "What happens if you get together? Will you be staying here or moving halfway across the country?"

"Good question." Shai nodded.

"What are we doing, talking about that potential possibility if I don't even know where this is going? Hell, I'm not sure it is going anywhere."

"Struck a nerve, she's starting to cuss, Tara."

Eva wanted to punch Shai for pointing that out. Not like Tara wouldn't have known anyway but still, it was the principle. "Let it alone," she snapped.

Both her sisters arched eyebrows at her. However, they dropped it.

An act that raised her own suspicion tenfold. She reached for her margarita when her phone buzzed. "Monroe."

"Hey, Doc, sorry to bother you, but we need you here. Tony Mensalli took a turn for the worse and they want to operate now."

Her own troubles vanished with a puff and she pushed back her chair. "He's not ready for surgery. Who wants to operate and what do you mean by 'he took a turn for the worse'?" Meeting her sisters' gazes, she knew they understood and would cover her bill. They waved as she grabbed her items and left, grateful she'd had her water first.

Jogging to her car, she slid behind the wheel and went hands-free as she headed for the hospital while her nurse filled her in on everything that had happened since she'd made her final rounds a couple of hours ago.

At the hospital, she hurried inside and to her locker. Changing shoes, she shoved into her slip-ons then shrugged into her white coat. As she left the staff room, the head nurse caught up with her.

"He's been prepped and is in the room now. Everything is ready for you to go in. Dr. Lopez is there, as well. He'll be performing the surgery unless some more cancer pops into view that hasn't shown up on the scans. We're still trying to ascertain where the bleeding came from. But he wanted you in there with him, since Tony is your cancer patient."

She lengthened her short stride, determined to get there. Dread filled her. They'd been hoping he would turn a corner and beat this but as of this moment, he hadn't accomplished that. Eva scrubbed in and was gowned and gloved within seconds. "Doctor," she said, entering the room.

"Thanks for coming, Dr. Monroe. I know you had left for the day."

"Thank you for requesting they call me in."

A lot of doctors had huge egos, and she understood that—hell, hers was healthy, nothing to scoff at—but in these types of situations, she had no problem thanking a doctor for doing something he didn't have to do.

It may not have been easy for her to take a back seat to this operation, but she held her tongue and did just that. Dr. Lopez was damn good at his job and found the bleeder, addressed it and sewed up Tony, all with the boy hanging in here.

Damn, this is nerve-racking when I'm not the one in control of the knife.

They departed and tossed their gowns in the bin.

"You've got a terrific hand, Dr. Lopez," she said. "Thank you for doing such a great job on him."

"He means a lot to you." The man looked at her with a smile.

"All my patients do. I see them at their most vulnerable and they are so young with so much life that should be ahead of them. I get attached, what can I say?"

"No, no. I think it should be that way. Too many doctors want to keep a distance and are more worried about their live versus die stats. They keep more than an arm's length, so nothing affects them. However, I think it does, anyway. They're so focused on remaining distant they leave off the most important part of being a doctor. The healing isn't just with medicine from a bottle or surgery. It comes from those around them, the love, the emotion."

"You are right about one thing, not many docs share that view. They're about getting people in and out of their office. Numbers mean money." She shrugged. "I may be exhausted, but I make it a point to always speak with the family and the children. I'm part of their lives and I should be near family. They are trusting me with their child's life."

"I would like to talk to you more about this but right now I have to go. My wife is on another floor in labor and I would like to be there for her."

"Oh, my God! Go, go. I'm sorry for running my mouth."

He smiled at her. "I'll see you later, Dr. Monroe." He hurried away, ripping the cap from his head.

Eva rubbed the small of her back and fought a yawn. She dug into her pocket and removed her cell, checking the time. Too late to call her sisters, so looked like it was time to head to an all-night diner and grab something to eat. Exchanging shoes once more, she then walked to her car and slipped behind the wheel.

Things would be so much different if I had a man waiting for me at home. Hell, if Grant was there, I may not have gone out with my sisters. Probably would have found something else to do there.

The roads were with minimum traffic, so she didn't have to waste a lot of time traveling to her familiar food spot. Once inside, she was met with smiles and waves from the staff who were used to seeing her. Snagging her typical booth, she accepted the coffee with a smile and placed her order as her stomach rumbled. She'd left her seafood on the table earlier and her belly was rebelling.

* * * *

Grant tapped his pencil on the desktop as he waited for his call to be answered. By the third ring, he was antsy. Fifth, about to give up but then he heard her voice.

"Dr. Monroe."

"Hello, beautiful," he said, smiling and reclining in his chair.

"Grant."

Was he mistaken, or was that surprise he had called? Angling his head to the side, he blinked then shook off those thoughts. "I'm sorry for bothering you, but I wanted to hear your voice."

"It's not a bother. How are you doing? How's your family?"

"We're okay. It's an adjustment not having him around. Mom still hasn't gotten back out there fully and she's canceled all her traveling for the rest of the year."

"I'm so sorry."

"It's part of life. She would like you to come out. She wants to spend some time with you and get to know you."

"She does?"

"Yes, I think part of her isn't sure she didn't imagine you there."

"Because of the blue in my hair?"

He laughed. "No, I think because I was holding your hand."

"Does that mean something else out in Arizona that I don't know about?"

"Yes," he deadpanned. "It means we're now married."

"Ahh, I see."

Grant imagined her nodding while her lips quirked up at the edges.

"And do they hand out these rules when you land at the airport, pass them out when you cross state lines?"

"No, we pick and choose when we want to implement them."

"Oh, so that's how it works."

He scratched his thigh. "Absolutely."

"Something specific you called for, Doctor?"

"Yes, I want to see you."

Her heavy sigh made him uncertain and he had nothing but disdain for the emotion.

"I'm sorry. I can't get away right now. I have a lot of surgeries lined up and I can't have anyone take them for me."

"I can come to you." He sat forward. "Let me do that. Let me fly to you and be there."

"I'm not saying you can't come out. In fact, I'd love to see you and I know my sisters would want to meet you. Although, that in itself should scare the shit out of you."

"I can't wait to meet your sisters. We have to talk about us and I want to do that face to face, not over the phone."

"Come on out. I'll even provide you with a room to stay in. Make sure to give you a good rate."

"Does it come with a roommate?" His cock thickened at the thought of being with her.

"It could. Do you have preferences?"

"Most definitely. I'd like a woman with curves in all the right places, sassy, spunky. A spiky blonde with sapphire-blue tips on her hair."

"Tall order. But I'll see what I can arrange for you." Muffled voices came from her end of the call. "I'll see you soon, Grant. I have to go right now. But, I will see you soon, Doctor." She was gone before he could say anything else.

Settled back in his chair, he started his Mac and bought himself an airline ticket. He wasn't about to screw around and not get out to her. He wanted this, whatever they had, to work. Sure, the sex had been explosive but there was more. And she'd proven that when she'd been at his side for his father's funeral.

His sister walked in his office as he just clicked the purchase button on his ticket. "Hey, Grant. Do you have a minute?"

"For you? Always." He half-stood until she waved him back to the chair. "What's going on?" Grant was a bit shocked at seeing her here, as she worked in a different hospital and didn't get here to this one often.

"I have a date tomorrow night and I wanted to know if you could spend dinner with Mom." She stretched out her legs and crossed her ankles. She wouldn't meet his gaze for longer than short sections of time.

"Date? Who is it with?"

Lucy scrunched up her face. "Really? We still have to do this?"

"Of course, we do. Just because you grew up, doesn't mean I am not going to be nosy and the protective older brother I've always been."

She glared at him.

He stared back, eyebrow arched.

With a huff, she drummed her fingers on the arm of his chair. "I can't believe that look still works on me. It's one of my colleagues. We're going to have a nice dinner. He's been asking me for a while and I've always come up with a reason not to go, but since Dad's passing, I'm looking at it like life is too damn short for me to not take some chances."

Grant understood that. He had a lot of the same thoughts. "I've been feeling that way, as well. So, yes, I will have dinner with her. I'm leaving the next week."

"I didn't think you went back to the Congo for a few more months."

"I don't, actually it's only one month. But right now, I'm heading to Iowa."

Lucy drew back. "What's in— Oh, the girlfriend you met in Mexico, right?" A wicked grin crossed her face. "Or have we not hit girlfriend status yet, despite her coming out here to support you at the funeral?"

"You can shut it now, Lucy, thank you."

"For a big brother, you sure are slow sometimes. Tell her how you feel, Grant. Don't put it off."

"I planned on it, thank you for the advice, though, Doc."

"Good." She stood and beckoned to him. "Now, come on. Take your favorite sister to lunch, she's hungry."

He got to his own feet and rolled his eyes. "Who said anything about you being my favorite? You're my only sister. I never said favorite."

"For that, this meal is going to include dessert." She frowned at him, despite the sparkle in her gaze.

He didn't mind. Seeing her laugh and smile again was worth all the dessert in the world. "Since I'm broke, I'll take you to the cafeteria."

She snorted and shook her head. "Hell, no. I want a nice meal, not whatever that crap is that's served there."

"So judgmental. You eat at your hospital."

"It's mine, this one is yours, not the same thing."

Grant slung his arm around his baby sister and together, they left his office. They agreed on a place and he led the way there, she followed behind in her Audi coupe.

Once he got home that night, he set up his Mac and used it to call Eva. He waited impatiently for her to answer and smiled the moment he witnessed her face come into view.

"Hello," he said. *Lord, she is beautiful.* Her long thick lashes were darker blonde than her hair and continually mesmerized him.

"Hi, Grant." She sat and crossed her legs on the couch. "You're looking well, getting some rest?"

"Some, yes. You?"

"You know how it goes. Some days are harder than others."

He did know that firsthand and nodded. "Want to talk about it?" His intention of calling her wasn't to talk shop but if she needed to, he would.

She worked her lower lip in her teeth.

Instantly, his groin tightened against his shorts, pushing the material, wanting to be set free. "No. I'm fine. I've had my margarita and was reading a book."

"Some sappy romance?"

"No, actually this was a murder mystery. It's good, too, kind of has a Stephen King, Dean Koontz feel to it as well. I like it, keeping me on the edge of my seat." Her tone was excited and it made him wonder what the name of the book was. If she sounded so happy to read it, perhaps it was something he would enjoy reading.

He ran his gaze along the graceful curve of her neck, remembering what it was like to have his face buried there, swipe his tongue over her skin tasting her, smelling the scent of pears that hung around her even after she climbed out of the ocean.

"What?" she asked. "Do I have something on my face?"

"No, why?"

"The way you're staring at me."

"No, I'm just remembering what it was like when we were in the same room and I could touch you, skim my hands over your curves. Hold your hips as I drive my cock into you over and over again."

Damn if her eyes didn't flutter and her chest move as she inhaled with a sharp breath.

Christ, he wanted her within reach.

"That's not fair," she moaned, shifting on her seat.

"Why not? It's the truth."

"You know, just for that, you're going to have to make it up to me."

Her flirtatious smile turned him on even more. "How can I do that?"

"Let me watch you jack off." She shifted once more before moving her screen a bit. "In fact, strip naked, lie on your bed and let me watch you wrap your hands around your beautiful cock and jerk it until you come. Let me watch you pleasure yourself."

The rasp in her voice damn near made him shoot his release. Grant ripped off his shirt and threw it to the side. Standing, he shucked his shorts and boxers. His dick stood out, hard and needing a wet pussy around it. Not just any but the woman he saw staring at his package from the computer screen. He lifted his Mac and went to his bedroom. Getting situated, he looked at her and said, "Aren't you getting undressed?"

"Do you need that in order to masturbate? You need me naked?"

"It's how I envision you when I do it. Need it? No. Want it, fuck, yeah." He grasped his cock as her fingers went to the first button on her shirt.

God, she was going to tease him and it was going to be hell.

"You stop jacking, I stop stripping," she warned, dragging her finger down between her breasts.

His dick jumped in his hand as he tightened his grip, working up and down once more. He wanted to see her shaved pussy, her playing between the lips as she fingered herself, and hear her mewls as she pushed herself over that edge. It would have to do until he got there next week.

Unfair but he was up to the challenge. He hoped. If not, Grant was about to embarrass himself in front Eva.

Chapter Eight

"Oh, fuck!" Eva screamed and bucked against the arm across her belly, holding her in place as he remained buried between her legs, eating her out. She couldn't move Grant's arm. He was too strong for her to do that. Her entire body was a mass of trembling nerves and she could only ride the onslaught of orgasms he applied to her body.

His tongue continued to flick against her clit as he thrust his fingers in and out of her. He used three, spreading her wide, filling her. She shuddered as another mini aftershock ripped through her.

"Please, Grant. Oh, for the love of – Put your dick in me, please?" She wanted it, wanted him deep inside her. And for that reason, she had no qualms about begging.

He pushed his fingers fully inside of her once more and rose over her until their lips were touching. "My fingers are there right now and don't want to leave." He wriggled them around a bit more.

Her lids lowered and she bit her lip. "You know I'm going to make you pay for this."

"No, this is me getting retribution for you making me jack off for you, staring at you while you played with my pussy, but I couldn't touch it."

She smiled at the recollection. "That was a fun night. I loved watching you jack off. In fact, I want to see it again."

"Not right now." He pushed forward with his fingers again. "Right now, I'm going to slide my cock in you, work it until you scream my name, then do it all over again. Then we're going to move to a wall or a counter until I'm finally sated, after all this time away from you."

She fairly purred. "Talk is cheap, Doc." If it took goading to receive his cock, so be it. That's what she would do.

He removed his fingers and while the frustrated whimper was on the edge of her tongue, she contained it, well aware of the broad head of his erection nudging against her opening.

Grant placed his fingers on her lips. "You do like pushing. Clean off your cream from my fingers. Suck them like you do my cock."

She curved her tongue around one digit, tasting herself on him as she swirled it around. "Can't argue with that. I do. I also like fucking. Can we get to that?"

He held her gaze without blinking and pushed his cock in her. One smooth, continuous slide until he stretched her and couldn't go any deeper. "Better?"

This time, she did purr. Hell, she must be part cat, given how it vibrated right from her throat. "Hell, yes." She locked her legs around his hips, holding him close and shifted, rolling her lower body, grinding on him.

He removed his fingers from her mouth, captured her hands and positioned them high above her head. Then he kissed her neck. Light fleeting kisses that only fanned the flames more. He didn't move, however, just held still, fully inside her, stretching her, his gaze locking onto her.

"What?" she asked. She wriggled her hips, trying again to get him to move.

"I love watching you as my dick is buried in you. Your eyes go all smoky and slightly unfocused." He brought his face a tiny bit closer to her. "You fit against me perfectly, Eva. And I fit in you perfectly."

"No argument here," she said, ignoring the way her belly fluttered at his phrasing. She shifted again, hoping he would move.

No such luck, he remained immobile, stretching her.

Raising up as much as she could with how he had her, Eva captured his lower lip in her teeth, nipping slightly. "Please move."

Without a word, he withdrew from her until just the head of his shaft remained inside her. Then he pushed forward again, not fast, not hard, just a continuous slow glide until he had sunk all the way within her once more.

His agonizingly slow strokes had the fire pumping through her veins.

Grant continued at his leisurely and toe-curling speed. Or lack thereof.

The fire slicing through her burned hotter than magma. Back and forth. In and out.

Clenching his hands, she hooked her legs around his waist, trying to keep him in deep. The tingling spiraled out from her gut, moving through her entire body.

Words escaped her as she submerged herself in what he created within her.

"Look at me."

Didn't even know I closed my eyes. She had. The command rode on a voice reminding her of *crème de menthe*. She lifted her eyes to his. Hell, the stare he leveled at her paired perfectly with the sex his voice alluded to. The sex he was delivering on.

He slid back then pushed forward one more time until he was unable to go any deeper. Grant released her hands and slid one down the side of her body. "I could stay here, forever."

His whispered words only fanned her flames of need.

"The way your pussy holds my dick, it's fucking heaven." A light brush of his lips. "Like this body was made for me."

She dug her fingers into his shoulders, content to let that occur. The purr in the back of her throat raced to the surface. Tugging her fingers through his hair, she arched closer, desperate for more skin-on-skin privilege.

He gave her more of his weight to hold. While he outweighed her by over a hundred pounds, she didn't mind in the slightest to be under him. Hell, if she could find a way to crawl into him and stay there, she would do just that.

Being between him and the mattress of her bed she couldn't think of a single place she would want to be instead of here. Or with anyone else.

Eva tightened her hold around his neck and turned her lips to him, sliding them along his cheek until they settled upon his. Then she slipped her tongue along the seam of his mouth before pushing past to seek out his organ and dance with it.

His groan rumbled up from his chest and she could feel it in her nipples.

Grant wrapped his arms around her, fingers splaying over the top of her ass and put them on their sides. Still buried deep inside her, he continued his lazy thrusting as he broke the kiss and held her gaze.

Christ, I'm in love with this man. The realization slammed into her and she jerked.

He canted his head to the side. "Eva? You okay? Did I hurt you?"

Scrambling her thoughts to form a coherent word, she pushed out a single one. "No." Mind racing, she added, "Cramp kicked in my leg."

He narrowed his gaze but didn't challenge her lie.

Thank God, he bought that. I seriously need to meet with my sisters and figure this out. She couldn't focus on it right then or she would freak the fuck out, so she locked it in a corner and allowed his touch to sweep her off again.

* * * *

"I'm not understanding what the problem is." Tara sipped her drink and shared a glance with Shai. "Are you?"

"Not in the slightest." Shai leaned forward and gestured at Eva. "Want to try again, Doc, for those of us who didn't understand the bullshit you just spouted?"

Drumming her fingers on the table, she huffed. "How can you not see the problem? I said I've fallen in love with him."

Her sisters shared another look.

Tara took up the mantle of speaker. "You had a fling with this guy that obviously meant more during that time than you allowed yourself to believe it did. We both knew that when you up and went to be at his side for his father's funeral. Nothing wrong with that. The sex is apparently off the charts because you shuffled in here with a few marks of scruff burn, I'm going to call it, on the side of your neck, and yet we've not met this man. So before we even get the chance to be face to face with him, you're telling us you love him. Not that you think you're falling in love but that you are in love with him." Tara shrugged. "There's not a damn thing for us to say."

Eva glanced to Shai.

"I agree with her. We love and support you, so if you love this man, why are you trying to find a way out of it? Love him. Be happy. We want to meet him but, sweetie, you don't need our permission to be in love." Shai took her hand. "Our job is to protect and love you, but if you feel this way about him, we're behind you."

Eva jerked her gaze between her sisters.

"You look like you're not sure who we are." Tara chuckled.

"I have to say, I was expecting some ribbing from you two on this."

"Look, we pick on you, tease you, harass you but when it comes down to it, we want you to be happy. Besides, if you get married and adopt some kidlets, I get a little niece or nephew to corrupt, umm, I mean spoil." Shai batted her eyes with a cheesy smile on her face.

"You were right the first time. Corrupt. I'm not talking marriage or kids, definitely not, but I'm scared he doesn't feel the same way." Cold water splashed over her. She couldn't have kids. She had to adopt. He wanted kids of his own, she was sure.

Her sisters shared another look and said at the same time, "So ask him."

Bless them for being so blunt. Eva picked up her margarita and drank. She would need another of these if she wanted to find the balls to tell him how she felt. She'd left Grant walking around the city, exploring while she met her sisters for a drink. Everyone was meeting for supper. Then the following night, she would take him home to meet her parents.

They joked and laughed while they ate. However, when she tried to steer the topic to how their vacations had gone, both women changed the subject rather swiftly.

There were stories there but she didn't press them since, at the rear of her mind, Eva wanted to get back to her place and find Grant.

* * * *

Grant swallowed hard as he held the door for Eva. They were on the way to grab a late dinner. He'd spent the day exploring the Quad Cites alone while Eva had been at work then met her sisters for a drink, that was a bit unnerving.

He'd just gotten back to her nice apartment when she'd returned. That had set off an entire new round of making out, a nap and a shower — which led to more sex — before they'd dressed and left to come here.

The steakhouse was casual and as he trailed her inside, his nose was slammed with the scent of steak. His stomach growled in anticipation. He continually sent her looks continuous times because she seemed different. Reserved in a sense, nothing major but he could feel it, feel her pulling away from him. Hand on the small of her back, he flexed his fingers, experiencing more of her exposed skin beneath his touch. So silken and smooth, he'd become increasingly tactile while being with this woman.

It was his last night here. Tomorrow morning early, he would fly back to Arizona to get ready for his trip to the Congo. True he wasn't leaving for a bit yet, but he still had things to do before he flew out. For the first time ever, he felt hesitant about heading out.

Eva walked in front of him, talking with their hostess, and he took in the image she presented. Just like that first moment he saw her walk by him in that damn bikini and sarong, he had no recourse to the amount of lust slamming into him.

Christ, I'm worse than a teenager with his hands on his father's porn stash.

His dick pressed in demanding fashion against the fabric of his boxer briefs, wanting out. Or rather — wanting in her.

Her gray dress hugged her curves and made his mind go down roads he needed to stay off of tonight if he wanted to behave himself. Coughing to cover his wandering mind, he shoved his hands into his pockets and glanced around the building. Families and couples both were eating and spending time together.

"Here you are," their hostess said, putting down the menus. "Your waiter will be over momentarily."

Grant held Eva's chair for her, inhaling deeply as she sank onto the seat before him. Then he pushed her closer. "Thank you," he said, only to be echoed by Eva. He moved around to his seat and occupied it, eyes on his dinner date, he sent her a smile. His cock pushed harder at her responding grin.

Once their drink orders had arrived, he shifted on the seat as she curled her lips around the straw of her unsweetened tea and drank.

"Christ, you make that hot."

She blinked her lashes and laughed. As usual, it brought a bigger smile to his face. Such joy was expressed in her laugh, he could feel her love of life. Made him fall for her more. And yet, he still maintained she was holding something back. It was almost forced.

Shit. His thought slammed his mind to a halt as the realization hit him. He'd fallen for this woman. Hard. Fast. Completely.

"You seem awfully quiet today. Did you not have fun exploring around here?"

It took a moment for him to kickstart his brain. "I did. I guess I'm just tired." He sent her a wicked grin. "Or thinking about something else."

She leaned forward, eyes locked on him and sent him another of her toe-curling smiles. "What would that be?"

"You and me. Naked. Engaging in all kinds of fun, adult activities."

"Like a coloring book? I hear that's an adult activity now. Supposed to be calming and relaxing."

He opened his mouth to respond when their waiter returned to take their order. The glint in her eyes altered him to the fact she knew the waiter had been approaching. He waited until they were alone once more.

"Do you have a *Kama Sutra* coloring book? I'll color the image then we can practice it and see how well it works."

She bit her lower lip and waggled her eyebrows. "Let's skip the coloring and just try some of them out."

Christ, she was a vixen. "I'm all for dragging you out of here."

"I can walk but I don't know, being carried out may be fun."

He had to force himself to remain seated. "I know you didn't eat much today and that's the only reason I'm not carrying you out now."

"Such a gentleman."

"Yeah, a fucking hero," he grumbled.

Eva slid her foot up the inside of his leg. "I promise I'll make it up to you. If it helps, I'm only wearing one article of clothing tonight."

Goddamn, motherfucking hero. His cock had far surpassed being ready to rebel and just punch free of his slacks. Grant drank some ice water hoping it would calm down his pulse and the heat coursing through him. All he could envision was her sitting there in nothing but that clingy dress. No bra. No panties. No barrier.

It didn't work.

Dinner was stressful for him. His dick remained painfully hard through the entire meal and dessert as he wanted nothing more than to put her across this table and fuck her until neither of them could walk straight. All while she'd dodged his questions of whether or not something was wrong.

After paying, he put his hand on the small of her back and guided her out the doors to her vehicle. Night had fallen and the lot was dimly lit where she'd parked. They walked around a bit before coming back to the car. He held the door for her and trapped her between him and the frame before she could slide behind the wheel.

Her blue eyes met his and he memorized her features. The shape of her face, her cheekbones, nose and lips, including the one dark mole on her lower lip to the left. The blue tips in her hair fit her personality. "Let's go," he whispered.

"Sure thing." Eva dragged one hand down his chest, allowing her nails to rake him.

Shuddering, he tried harder to rein in the beast clawing at his soul to get out and take her. Closing the door on her, he walked around to the passenger side and climbed in.

His heart kicked up in speed when she reached out for his hand and laced their fingers together. There wasn't any way he was willing to give all this up.

She clasped his hand and released him.

Grant was about to protest when her touch landed on his cock and gave that a gentle squeeze. "Shit," he muttered, his shaft thickening even more if that were somehow possible.

"I promised I would make it up to you."

He gazed over at her in the dim lights from her dashboard, barely able to make out her features as she wasn't watching him but the road. Still, her fingers hadn't stopped, as she moved them up and down on his cock, stroking him through the slacks.

"You're driving." Crap, his words were all guttural and rasped.

"Yes, I am. I'm capable of doing more than one thing at a time." To prove her point, she undid the clasp of his pants and lowered his zipper. "See." Never once did she weave along the road.

Grant bit the inside of his lip as she took him out and purred.

He gripped the edges of the seat and gritted his teeth as she stroked.

Up and down his length, she moved her warm touch. Her thumb swiped along the swollen head, smearing the precum.

"This is not fair."

"It's not supposed to be. This is about me touching you. Not the other way around. Want me to stop?"

"Fuck, no." Grant covered her hand with his and increased the pressure around his dick.

She kept up her torture all the way back to her place and the moment she parked her car, he was reaching for her. Seconds later, he had her settled over his lap, his cock slipping fully into her, protected by the condom he'd put on while she turned off the engine.

She didn't verbalize anything, just sighed heavily as she placed her forehead on his. Right there in her car, he fucked her, oblivious to the outside world. Nothing mattered more than Grant and Eva. This was what he wanted in his life.

Eva.

Now, he just had to find a way to make it so. Flexing his fingers on her ass, he drove up into her, needing to claim, to mark, to make sure she never forgot him and didn't want anyone else.

As she kissed him, Eva rocked on his lap increasing the friction caused between the two of them.

Chapter Nine

"I'm heading to the Congo."

Eva pivoted around to the man behind her by the front window to her apartment. Grant wore a pair of black sweats and nothing else. His tanned torso didn't depict a man who spent his days indoors away from the sun. He was fit and a beautiful sight to behold.

Shoving her lust to the back corner, she zeroed in on his words. Her heart sank. The Congo. Not exactly ideal for a long-distance relationship. *I doubt we'd be able to talk on a regular basis even. But perhaps this is for the best. I've gotten too serious, this will give me the time to remember it's just sex between us. Nothing more serious, nothing permanent.*

She swallowed. Twice. Then forced a smile. *I have to be supportive.* She didn't want to, no, she wanted to demand he stay here with her. But that wouldn't work. He would want to talk future, which would lead to children, he would leave when he found out she couldn't have any. "When do you leave?"

He sliced his blue gaze to her as he moved in her direction. "The week after I return from here."

Nine days from now, as I've been obsessing that's he is only here for two more days.

He stood in front of her and she plucked at his waistband, avoiding eye contact, afraid of what it would expose. "For how long?"

"Two months."

Damn. Damn. Fucking god dammit! "I see." Eva was proud her voice didn't waver even in the slightest.

He gripped her upper arms and drew her in closer. "I want this to work out between us, Eva."

Splaying her hands on his chest, she pursed her lips then met his gaze. "Long-distance relationships are difficult, anyway. Add to that both our—" Her words fell away when he covered her mouth with one large palm. She experienced the sweetest urge to flick her tongue along his palm, if only to distract him from this talk.

"Don't give us reasons we can't work out."

"I'm being logical." She pushed the words out from behind his hand. *I'm trying desperately to protect my heart. Begin pulling away now so when you learn I can't have children your leaving doesn't hurt me as much as it will if I allow you to continue getting closer to my heart.*

He stepped away with a growl of frustration. "Nothing about our relationship has been logical from the jump, Eva. Meeting in a hotel in Mexico and having it carry over from the sex there. Most people have flings and leave, forgetting and not seeing that other person ever again. But not us." He raked a hand through his hair. "We did. You were there for me when my father died. I'm here now, visiting you. That alone proves there's more there." A shrug. "Here, whatever."

"The Congo seems so far away."

"It is. I didn't say it would be easy, Eva. Relationships take work. But I'm willing to try if you are."

Eva didn't have faith in relationships. At least not for her. They hadn't ended well so far. She exhaled slowly and stared at the man lounging before her, arms crossed over his chest as he waited.

Chewing on the inside of her cheek, she shrugged. "So how do you communicate while over in the Congo? Phone calls? Skype?"

"I have Skype on my laptop, yes. That would work fine. It's rural, yes, but we have good gear when we head over there."

"And the time difference?"

He stepped close again, running his fingers down the side of her face. "We'll figure it out, Eva. Stop trying to find reasons it won't. Allow us the chance to make it work out."

"Okay."

His smile did wicked things to her lady parts and she fought the urge to squirm. She just wanted to go back to bed with him and forget the rest of the outside world existed. Wrap up in his arms and just be with this man.

Why the hell am I refusing to push him away?

From the look in his eyes, he had the same idea. They'd gotten three steps when her cell rang.

"Shit," she muttered before diverting her direction to where she'd left it on the counter. "Dr. Monroe."

"Dr. Eva Monroe?"

"Yes. Who is this?"

"My name is Detective Coleman and I'm with Major Crime."

She stepped back from Grant and crossed her arms, confused. "Why are you calling my phone, Detective?"

"I'm calling about your sister, Tara."

Dread slammed into her and her limbs shook. "Tara?"

Grant moved up behind her, acting as her support as her legs were close to giving out. She leaned into him grateful he was there. "What happened to my sister?"

"She's at Trinity Methodist Hospital. She's been shot."

Her legs did give away and she would have hit the floor if not for Grant's arms around her, keeping her anchored to his strong body. "I'm on my way." She took Grant's hand before she dashed for her bedroom and shoved into clothing without paying much attention. The detective was on the phone explaining the situation and she responded with grunts. "I'll see you when I get there, Detective."

"I can have a car bring you."

"No time. I'm on my way out the door now. Thanks for the call."

Grant matched her step for step as she hurried. "Do you want me to drive?" His question came as they neared her car.

"No."

"Very well." He didn't argue with her just slid into the passenger seat.

Eva called Shai on the way. "Did you hear about Tara?" Her question fell in lieu of any greeting.

Her sister grunted before a not so muted swear filled the line. "Some Detective Coleman is on the other line, he said he has someone going to pick up Mom and Dad. Where are you?"

"Speeding to the hospital. You?"

"Same. Talk there."

Tears burned her eyes and she blinked them away with furious determination. "Yes." Wiping the traitorous ones that escaped, she focused on the road and wove around people, like they were standing still.

Screeching into a parking spot, she hurried from the car and ran for the doors, Grant on her heels. Once inside, the smells from the hospital slammed her and she stopped as if she'd hit a brick wall.

"Eva?" His deep voice slid around her like a warm, velvety blanket.

She held up a hand and took a moment to gather herself. Then she walked to the counter where a harried woman worked. "Yes?" she asked.

"I received a call my sister had been shot and brought in. Her name is Tara Monroe. Could you please tell me where she's at right now?"

"Surgery. Fifth floor, the doctor will be out to tell you what he knows when he can."

Biting back her snippy response, Eva nodded. "Thank you."

As they walked to the elevator, Grant slid his hand in hers and she gratefully accepted his strength.

"You handled that well."

"I work in a hospital. I know it's not the best way to get information by yelling and screaming at them. They work hard, too."

"I know but a lot of people wouldn't have cared." He gathered her close once they were in the elevator.

"Honestly, I don't think I would have but the smell snapped me out of my daze and reminded me where I was."

The silver doors slid open and they stepped out onto the floor. She glanced around the waiting room and sighed. She was the first to arrive so she picked a spot on one of the couches.

Grant sat next to her, his arm along the back, fingers caressing her shoulder.

A few moments later, Shai hurried in, her heels clacking on the floor.

Eva stood and rushed to hug her sister.

"Any news?" Shai questioned as she accepted a hug from Grant as well. "Tell me what you know." Shai's tone was demanding.

Eva understood her anxiety. This was their sister in there. "Nothing yet. I just got here a minute ago."

Tensions were high and ratcheted up further when their parents arrived. Sourness filled her gut as she saw the strain on everyone's face. She offered to get coffee and she left before anyone could say no.

Grant accompanied her. "You hanging in there?"

"I hate not knowing. I want to go in and demand answers. It's so damn different when it's someone else in there that's not my family."

He draped an arm around her shoulders and dropped a swift kiss to her temple. "I know."

Yes, she understood he knew, given what he'd recently gone through with his own father. "I want to make it better for them, be able to tell them in layman's terms what's going on with her. Her prognosis and just—everything." Her voice broke on that last bit and she clamped her mouth shut.

Grant didn't speak, but nodded. He left her there and put in the order for coffee, giving her a moment to get herself together.

While she waited, she prayed that her sister would be fine.

In the back of her mind, Eva realized she had to keep her focus on her family and not men who would come and go.

While it wasn't a fair to this guy with her to lump him in to all the others who had a Y chromosome, but life wasn't fair.

* * * *

Congo

Grant wiped his hand across the gathered sweat on his forehead, smearing it along his skin. Patience hadn't ever been his strong suit and now as he watched time tick away, he wanted to push it along until he could call Eva. He'd been here for a week and wanted nothing more than to talk to her and hear her sexy voice in his ear. It was the next best thing aside from having her with touching distance. He'd never met a woman he wanted to be more tactile with than her. And he had no desire to look for another.

She'd left him a text informing him that her sister was doing better but it wasn't enough. It never was until her voice rang in his ear. He strode across the compound to his room, determined to get directly out of this oppressive humid subtropical heat, at least for a little bit.

He snagged a bottle of water and after uncapping it, downed over half with a satisfied groan. Rolling his shoulders, he walked to the chair by the window and sank to the holey cushion. He wasn't about to complain there were holes in it. Hell, he was happy he had an extra chair in his room. It didn't always happen that way. So he would take it. Feet stretched out in front of him, he closed his eyes.

The buzzing of his phone jolted him awake and he scrambled for it as he shook off the sleep that had snuck up and claimed him. "Dr. Harrison."

"Did I interrupt something important? You sound out of breath."

"Eva, no, dear God no. I dozed off. You're not interrupting anything. How are you? It's good to hear your voice. How is Tara doing?" He didn't have any way to explain the warm fuzzies that coursed through him at the mere sound of her voice. Honestly, he didn't believe he needed one either. This was just how it was, this woman was the one for him.

"I'm fine, staying busy. Good to hear your voice as well and Tara is recuperating. Never knew how damn difficult it was to keep an adult in bed."

He cocked a brow at her comment. Seconds later, her laughter had him smiling.

"Shit, not how I meant for that to have sounded. I mean, the children, we tell them they have to stay and they do. With Tara, Christ, I'd kill her if she were my patient. I mean just today, I caught her on her way out the door, bitch actually thought she was going sneak out to head into work."

He reached for his water and drank while she ranted about her sister.

It took a few moments for her to take a deep breath and continue with, "I'm sorry, you don't need to hear this crap."

"No, I love it, truly. It's nice to hear things from home."

Silence lingered between them for a moment.

"How are things there?" Her question came on a thread of voice huskier than usual.

"Hot, humid. Busy, unfortunately. But going well, considering we're in a developing country that has many issues with government and warlords."

"Are you in any danger, Grant?" This time, her words were lined with fear.

It ate at his gut to hear this emotion in her voice. "I would be lying if I said no, because there is always going to be some danger in these poor countries. So, I won't lie. I will say that there is a large group of us and we take every precaution we can to stay safe."

Her silence damned. He cleared his throat.

"I'm glad you're staying safe. Are you with a good group?"

He nodded and spoke as he realized she wasn't right there with him. "I am. Most I've been out with before, there are only a few new people. We've got some specialists, dentists and surgeons here, so we're a well-rounded bunch of people."

"And people hook up?"

Grant knew where this conversation was heading and rubbed his temple. "Eva, I told you. I wanted a relationship with you. Not anyone here. I don't care if we're over seven thousand miles apart. No one here has anything I want, could want, or will want."

"If you're sure."

"You're going to have to trust me on that, baby." He hated the uncertainty in her voice, but she was going to have to trust him.

"Right."

While part of him wanted to push that there were eligible men where she was and ask if anyone was interesting to her, he dropped it. That wouldn't help this issue fade, but push it to the forefront of her mind. He finished off his water and crossed his ankles. "Tell me what's going on over there. How's the weather because it's hot as fuck over here. I'm sure I'm losing weight just by being here."

"Cool right now. We took the kids who could go out to the garden area and brought in some therapy dogs to visit them. A good day for many."

"And those who couldn't go out?"

"Dogs were also visiting inside. We get a lot of volunteers to bring their animals by for these children to see and pet, or cuddle and hug. Does wonders for their morale and by that token, it also assists the parents who aren't used to seeing their children smiling and laughing."

There it was. The love in her voice. The proof she was going to be one hell of a mother and dote on her children. If she was so giving with her time for the children of other people. He closed his eyes and instantly an image of a pregnant Eva popped into his mind.

The gentle swell of her belly as she rested her hand on it. Wearing one of his oversized shirts, so he was covering both his women. It would be a girl. The first one at least. He wanted three. Seemed like it would be a great number.

"How are your parents doing?"

"Mom wants Tara to quit the DA's office since she got shot because of who she was prosecuting." A sharp bark of laughter. "Like that's going to happen, Tara isn't going anywhere. She refuses to be scared by something like that."

He sat forward. "It was due to a case?" He'd had to head over here before they found out as to why she'd been shot. However, that detective was hard on the case. It was big news when an ADA was shot.

"Yes, she's in the middle of prosecuting a corrupt owner of a construction company who has ties to the mob. Turns out he had a hit put out on her. So now, all of us have protection following us around. Good for my parents because it puts their mind at ease but annoying for myself and Shai. She doesn't like having anyone over her shoulder at work and it's really hard to convince a family to trust me with the life of their child when I have some hulking cop behind me. They don't exactly smile a lot."

"So you have a guy on you?"

"I wouldn't exactly put it that way, there's no guy on me, but yes, I do have a detail shadowing me. Tara insisted the family be protected."

"Then it's a woman."

"Now, you sound jealous, Grant. The one shadowing me is a man but he's happily married with five children. And the one who replaces him, if he is unable to be there right then in the middle of the night and I have to go, is a rookie who is young. Point being, I know I have to trust you, but that street goes both ways."

Duly chastised, he grunted. "Point taken." He rose and lumbered to the window where he peered out over the scenery he had. No denying his impressive view. Off in the distance, he could see the fog moving over the hills toward them along the Lualaba River. The rich variations of greens a striking difference than what he was accustomed to living in Arizona. The sights were well worth the humidity he had to endure. "I can't wait to show you the pictures I've taken, Eva. It's stunning here."

"Is this the last trip you're taking this year?"

"I'm not sure. I have the opportunity to go to South America later on. Haven't thought about it all yet. Was going to be making a decision while I was here. Why?"

"Was just curious what you were going to be doing for Christmas this year."

"Something you were planning?" He hoped she was, for he would love to see her and the sooner the better.

"Was thinking it would be nice to be with you at least part of the time. I know that you need to be there for your mother given what happened with your father this year."

"I'd like to see you too."

Noises exploded behind her and for a moment, he didn't hear her until the click of a door shut it all out.

"What's going on?"

"Mindy's birthday. We doctors know how to party but we get loud." Some light laughter. "You know how it is."

He agreed with that. "Don't you need to be with them?"

"It'll still be her birthday when I am off the phone with you. And she has the full day. It's only six in the morning here."

Which explained why he was so damn hot, it was noon in the Congo. "Did your shift change?"

She laughed and he smiled again, warmed just by that simple act.

Grant propped a shoulder against the window and stared out over the peaceful view as he listened to Eva talk. He may be unable to be with her, but this wasn't bad. Her voice in his ear and this stunning visual display to overlook. So long as no conflicts broke out, he was happy.

I'd be happier if she was here with me.

Until he could hold her again in person, Grant would relish these moments of connecting with Eva on the phone.

Chapter Ten

"So you're not coming for Christmas?" Eva struggled to control her temper as she paced before the blazing fire in her hearth.

"I'm sorry, Eva. I can't. I'm..." Grant cleared his throat. "Not in the country."

She ground her jaw and took several deep breaths. "I'm sorry, what? Where are you?"

"Uruguay."

She had the strangest urge to reach around to her back and pull out the blade sunk between her shoulder blades. There had to be one there for she sure as shitting felt the pain caused by his betrayal. It wasn't a feeling that she enjoyed in the slightest.

Flicking her tongue along her lower lip, she ambled to the window and stared out at the falling snow. The thick fat flakes dropped at a rapid rate, accumulating on the ground.

"I see." She forced her fingers to relax from the fist she'd had. "And how long have you been there?"

A moment of silence before he spoke. "Four days."

Betrayal. This was what it tasted like and she could honestly say she wasn't a fan.

"Eva? I know what I said about coming to see you for —"

Eva cleared her throat. "Don't worry about it. You made your choice. I think we should just end this all the way around. It was fun while it lasted but we both had to know it wasn't going to go anywhere, seriously. Goodbye, Grant." She ended the call before the tears began to fall.

She barely made it to her couch before her legs gave out on her. Tossing her cell away from her, she alternated between sadness and anger. Eventually anger won out. "The fuck he couldn't tell me before he left. I spent all this time getting everything ready and now he tells me he has been out of the goddamn country for nearly a week?" She slammed her hand on the arm of her couch, wincing as pain zagged up her arm.

Beside her, the buzzing from her phone snatched her attention, but when she saw Grant's name on the caller ID, she swore and pushed it away. Glancing around her apartment, she took in all the Christmas decorations she'd taken the time to put up, not wanting him to come and see an empty apartment. She didn't decorate much but wanted this to be special for him. Took an extra day off work to make sure all was as nice as she could make it.

Her mom decorated and had a flair for it, making it stunning, but she, it took a lot for her to create the atmosphere she desired.

All for not — because he wasn't coming. Not just that but he knew he wasn't coming and didn't believe she was important enough to give her that bit of information.

Her phone rang again and she walked away from it, only to whip back and pull it close. Going into contacts, she marked his ring tone, so she would know when he called. Temper riding high, she was close to ripping down all the merry decorations she'd painstakingly put into place.

She took a deep shuddering breath. Stalking up to the first silver tinsel garland she could reach, she curved her fingers around it, ready to yank, then hesitated. *Why let him ruin this for me? I decorated, I like how it looks, I'm having my sisters over tonight. I am damn well going to enjoy this.*

Perhaps not as much had he been there to share it with her, but she hadn't let a man dictate her happiness before and she'd be damned if she started now. Determination stamped in her bones, she headed to the kitchen where she began making some Irish coffees, her sisters would be here soon, and she knew they would want one.

She even had the proper glasses to serve them in and she made a damn impressive drink. It was one of the few things she'd managed to retain from her only trip over to Ireland. Once the glasses were down, she started on the coffee. She grabbed down the brown sugar and whisky, then staged for her setup.

The door opened, bringing in her siblings, and she smiled at them as they shrugged out of their heavy coats and shook the snow from their hair.

"Cold as fuck out there. I'm ready to head back to Mexico. Who's with me?"

Eva shook her head at Tara's comment. "You do realize you'd have to go back out in the cold to get to the airport."

"Stop ruining my pipe dream, you evil whore."

Shai rolled her eyes and walked in the kitchen. "Coffee ready?"

"Making it now," she said, grabbing the three glasses and added steaming hot water to them to pre-heat them. "Just waiting on the coffee to finish. Check on dinner, will you?"

Shai went to the oven and checked on the cheddar-baked chicken in there. "Looks good to me. So do the beans. Not much longer."

"I love what you've done to the place, Eva. Care to come over and do mine?"

"No, thank you, Tara. I almost tore it all down a bit ago."

"Why?" both siblings asked that simultaneously.

She flicked her tongue along her lower lip and sighed heavily. "I called him to see how he was and when I could expect him to arrive. He then informed me that he wasn't coming and had been out of the country for four days. He's hanging out in Uruguay." She prepped the cream to its proper half-whipped state. "Apparently whatever they are offering in Uruguay is so much better than anything I could have possibly come up with here in the American Midwest." Eva heard the hurt in her tone but tried not to make it sound worse than it was, tried to show that her heart hadn't shattered into all those tiny insignificant pieces.

"The fuck you say?" Shai whirled around and crossed her arms as she stood before the stove.

"And he didn't say anything beforehand?" Tara curved her hand into a fist.

Lord help her, she loved her sisters. "Nope, I just found out when I called him. So I hung up on him and that's it, we're done." Hell, even saying the words hurt her heart. She'd fallen for him, hard. *And as predicted, got my heart busted in the process. Oh, well, live and learn.*

They both hugged her. "Thanks. It is what it is. Sucks, but I'll move on." Taking the coffee, she added it then mixed until the sugar melted into the brew. Next came the whiskey and she added equal amounts to each, then looked at her sisters as she waited for the brew to still. "I really liked him, too." Tears burned her eyes and she prayed they wouldn't fall. "But it's better this way."

"I know you did," Tara said, squeezing her shoulder. "Why do you say that?"

"Because we know I can't have children and men want to have their own."

Her sisters glared at her.

She set her jaw and looked away not wanting to argue about that statement, plus she had more tears threatening. Picking up the hot spoon and the whipped cream, she slowly poured it over the back of the spoon. By the time she finished, she smiled at her artwork.

"Perfect," she said. Sliding a glass to each sister, she lifted hers by the stem. "Drink up."

They all hoisted their drinks.

"To family," Eva said.

Her sisters echoed her and they clinked glasses.

She took her first drink and moaned as the concoction streamed down her throat, warming her from the inside out.

"You make a killer drink, sis."

"Thanks, Shai. It's the one thing I remember from Ireland. Learned from an old man in the back of a small pub."

Her sisters kept up small talk during the meal, avoiding any mention of the man who was no longer coming for the holiday.

Eva made them each another drink after they ate dessert then they sat around her fireplace, classical music in the background, and just enjoyed the company they provided.

"So," Shai said, after she took a big drink of her coffee. "What are we telling Mom and Dad about the rat bastard who now isn't coming?"

Eva loved their unwavering support. "I'm going to tell them the truth, he's out of the country, doing what he does." Even as the calm words fell from her mouth, her fingers clenched around the stem of her mug. "I'll let them know later tonight."

Tara finished her drink and slumped down in her oversized chair, looking almost like a child in an adult's seat. She dangled her legs over and moved them back and forth, not at all appearing like the cutthroat ADA she was. Recovering from a gunshot wound or not, she still looked like a little kid. "Stop laughing at me," Tara demanded. "I know what you're thinking."

"If you did," Eva said, trying her best to contain her mirth, "you wouldn't be sounding like a petulant brat."

"She *is* a brat," Shai chimed in.

"Fuck the both of you."

"Do you kiss your mother with that mouth?" Eva teased.

"I do, thank you very much," she sassed back.

"And the bastard when he calls back, again?" Shai ground out her question.

"Let it go, Shai."

"I would but your phone keeps lighting up with his name in the display. You shouldn't have left it by me, if you didn't want me to speak on it."

Grumbling at her sister, she slid off the couch, swiped her phone from the end table and tossed it to a seat no one was in, or by. "Happy now?"

"Not really," she said. "But this isn't about me, it's about you and Mr. McHottie-Asshole."

Eva had been lucky throughout dinner but now the gloves were about to come off. She settled in for the imminent grilling session.

* * * *

Grant swore again, as he tried Eva back once more. Nothing, all he got was her voicemail. Not even a pick up, then hang up. She wasn't even accepting his calls.

It's not like I didn't want to be there with her. But it's more than that. She said we were finished for good. Over. Finite.

"What's up, man?" one of the other doctors popped their head in the room and asked. Daniel Horowitz was an amazing doc but not at all the person he wanted to discuss his relationship issues with. Hell, he wasn't sure he had a relationship anymore.

"Calling home," he said, waving the phone before him.

"When you're done, a few of us are in the front playing poker if you'd like to join us." He backed out and vanished from view.

Poker, not exactly the act he wanted to partake in, either. Still, it was thoughtful to be invited and he did get along with this group of doctors.

Regardless, he tried to get through to Eva once more. The just like all the times before it went straight to voicemail. "Eva, please call me back. I know I should have handled this better but don't make it be the thing that comes between us. Let's talk about this." A moment's pause. "Please. I don't want this to end."

He dropped the phone and cradled his head in his hands. "I've fucked up the best thing to stroll into my life." His fault, he ran when he was too close to something. Using his need to help others as an excuse.

Yet for the life of him, he couldn't explain why he had chosen to head to South America instead of Iowa.

"That's easy."

He jerked his head up and found himself staring at Denise Carter another of the doctors with them.

"Excuse me?"

She walked in and sat on one of the empty chairs as if she owned the place. "You were muttering about you weren't sure why you came here, instead of going to Iowa." She shrugged. "I said that's an easy answer."

"No offense, Denise, but I'm really not in the mood."

She shrugged easily. "Of course not, men never are. But then, you'll sit there and wonder until it gets to anger then it starts to be her fault and you're never with her again, because you're both angry and you refuse to accept the simple reason as to why you avoided going there in the first place. So fine, sorry for disturbing you." Denise rose and walked back to the door she'd just entered through moments prior.

"No, wait."

She gazed back at him over her shoulder. "What?"

"What exactly do you know that's so easy I'm overlooking it?"

She faced him, eyebrows raised.

He beckoned to her, inviting her closer. "I mean it, I want to know."

Denise strode to the nearest chair and straddled it, putting her arms on the back. "You came here because while it's still a coward's way out from progressing your relationship, you're still doing something helpful. It's simple. You're scared of taking this next step with her, so you back out of spending the holidays with the woman and her family. That's a big thing to do, no denying it. But you didn't want to remain in the States and just be like, well, I decided not to come, so you volunteered for this last minute, because it's still a worthy cause. And you can give yourself so many different excuses as to why you did. They needed your help because they were short doctors, or whatever. Bottom line is, you're not in the country, so your family can't push you to go and you can't just up and show up. Then again, neither can she just jump on a plane and come to you."

Those words hit the truth mark with unerring accuracy. *Shit*.

"So you understand?"

She narrowed her eyes slightly. "Don't get it twisted. I think you're a prick for what you did. I just said it was easy to point out the reason. But, no, I don't understand why you did it. Especially, if you didn't give her any warning you were coming out to this location until you were here, which from the expression on your face, you didn't do." Denise scuffed her feet on the floor a few times. "Listen, I dated a man like you once. Good man, no denying it and we had fun together. For all intents and purposes, I thought we were moving in a certain direction, but he continued bailing during certain things we planned. Oh, sure, when we were together he would say all the right things and do them as well, but I couldn't help but wonder. And he pulled something like what you're doing."

"And did you give him another chance?"

"Me? Fuck, no, that was the end of it for me. But he'd done it several times before. He called after that wanting to talk, wanting me to forgive him. I did. I forgave him, I let go of the anger." She narrowed her eyes. "I also let go of him."

His heart plummeted. "She'll talk to me."

Her smile didn't offer him a single shred of comfort but then neither did the blank expression she leveled in his direction.

"Sure, she will." Denise left him alone.

Grant thought about her words and realized she had him pegged. He always thought about a future with Eva but when this got there, he ran. Cold feet.

"I'm such a fucking pussy." He headed for his room and flopped back on the bed, all the while cursing himself into the next century. Grant lay there for about five minutes before he got to his feet and went to join the poker game.

The guys welcomed him and got him a drink.

They played into the night and he headed back to his bed, buzzed and horny. Closing the door behind him, he took care of his needs then flopped into bed, still horny and still feeling the effects of his drinking. Fumbling for his phone, he pulled up pictures of him with Eva.

"Eva," he muttered, stroking his thumb down the image.

So full of life, so vibrant. So his.

"At least then."

He pulled up her contact information and pressed the call button. It rang and rang then went to voicemail again. Buzzed, yes, drunk enough to leave a rambling message on her phone? No. He hung up and let it fall to the mattress beside him.

Falling asleep on this narrow cot wasn't ideal, not when he knew he had a queen-sized bed he could have been in...with a willing woman.

His frustrated groan was dragged out from his chest as he gripped his balls and tugged gently. Far too long since he'd had her touch on him. And that's what he wanted. He ran his hand over his cock and balls, increasing the pressure as he did it over and over again, never once picking up his dick, yet just using the flat of his palm. Over the shaft then down along his sac and back up again.

Grant closed his eyes and pretended Eva lay there with him, her touch, her hair skimming along his chest. He tugged on his balls once more before actually curving his hand around his shaft. He drew down and away from his body as more blood pumped through to gather in his cock. Once it grew fully erect, he sped up his strokes, short fast pumps as he massaged his balls with his other hand.

He focused on the blonde before him, with the blue tips in her hair as she played with her wet pussy while he jerked off. This act turned her on so much, she'd told him that more than once. He loved watching her masturbate, watching her show him what felt good to her, letting her tease herself as he was having to do right this moment.

Adjusting his grip so his thumb was up and not down toward his groin he fisted faster, pinching the head to extend his pleasure. His balls drew tight and he yanked harder, needing the release, craving it so he could then relax and possibly get some sleep.

His cum shot out of him some hitting his abs and some leaking down over his hand. It would suffice for now, but not as much pleasure as when Eva was with him. Grant cleaned himself up all the while thinking about how he was going to go about getting her back into his life.

He had a lot of work to do once he made it back Stateside. But this time he wasn't going to be running away like a coward. He would get his woman, claim her and keep her.

Grant didn't get much sleep for about two hours after he lay down. Then they woke him for an emergency that had arisen. As he shrugged into his shoes, the thought once more about the surgeon he'd left behind in Iowa.

The hell he was giving her up without a fight.

Chapter Eleven

"Dr. Monroe you have a call on line four. Dr. Monroe, line four."

She smiled down at the boy whose room she was in at the moment. "Excuse me, Taylor, I have a call to take. I'll be right back."

"What about our game?" He watched her with those big brown eyes.

"Well, it's your turn, so you figure out your next move and I'll be right back in."

"Promise?"

She cupped his face, his dark brown skin soft and still a bit clammy. "I promise." She exited his room and went to the nearest phone, grabbed the receiver and pressed the proper button. "This is Dr. Monroe."

"Dr. Monroe, this is Archibald Quintero down at the Santo Domingo Children's Cancer Society in Orlando. We spoke earlier this year about you coming down to give a talk on some of your procedures done at your facility."

"Yes, sir, I recall that conversation. Good to hear from you." That had happened before her vacation to Mexico and Grant. She shook off that memory and focused on the man at the other end of the call. "How can I help you today?"

"We were wondering if you had some time to come down in January. I know it's not a lot of advanced notice, but we were just able to get everything in order. Is this something you think you would be able to do?"

She pulled out her phone and called up her schedule. "Let me take a look. What dates were you considering specifically?" While she didn't think it would be an issue, she wasn't positive.

It didn't take long, and she verified the dates in question were free for her to go down to Orlando.

"Thank you so much. We've heard such amazing things coming from your hospital and we're looking forward to implementing some of them into our work."

"It's my pleasure. And I will see you in two weeks. Thank you for getting me out of Iowa for part of the winter." This season had come in with a vengeance and was making her ever regret not once taking a position in a state where they didn't have to deal feet of snow and ice in the winter. While it wouldn't be heading to Mexico the temperature of Florida when she watched the Weather Channel was hellaciously better than anything she had in her forecast currently.

His laugh sounded kind and welcoming. "Our pleasure. Thank you."

Eva hung up and walked back into Taylor's room where he watched for her with expectant eyes. "Ready?" she asked with a smile.

He nodded and beckoned to her. "I went, now it's your turn. I waited for you a little bit then because you weren't here, I took another turn."

She settled beside him. "Two turns in a row? Okay, let's see what happens now." She studied the checkers board and made her moves.

The smile on his face was worth everything to her. Damn if she didn't want to scoop him up and hold him tight.

Later that night, she was at her parents'. Her sisters were also in attendance and shot her sympathetic gazes when their parents were looking.

Her father squeezed her shoulder as he walked by carrying the pitcher of water for the table. "I'm sorry your young man didn't make it, but I'm glad he's helping people."

She bit her cheek to keep her anger contained and ensured that none of it leaked out into her tone. She had to be careful because her parents would pick up on it in a heartbeat. "Yes, me too." Her sisters met her gaze and it irked her to see sympathy in their eyes, not because she didn't believe it was real, but because if he'd been a man, this wouldn't have happened to begin with. "I got a call from the cancer society down in Orlando and they've set a date they'd like me to come down and share some of our practices."

Her family turned their attention to her. This type of singular focus from her family, she could handle. She was good at her job and had no problems talking to people about this.

"When would this be?" Ever the ADA her sister, always with the questions.

"Right after New Year's." She placed the basket of rolls down that she'd held in her hand. "He, Mr.

Quintero, just called me today and asked if I was available. I cleared it with Tony who says it's a great idea for me to go. So I'll be down there for about a week. Perhaps longer if I think I want to stay warm." She gave a pointed look out the window to where the conditions had turned to whiteout. Eva gave another thought to the fact this was one of the worst winters they'd had on record for well over two decades.

"Congratulations, honey," her mom said with a warm smile. "I'm sure you'll help them out a lot down there."

She returned the gesture before clearing her throat. "That's the plan, anyway. Just wanted to let you know because I'll be getting all ready on this end for the doctor who's covering for me. Unfortunately, what that is going to mean then is a lot of late nights and I'm sorry to say, no family dinners until after I get back."

Thankfully they understood, may not like it, but they definitely understood.

After they finished the filling meal and dessert, she stood with her sisters in the kitchen doing dishes with Tara while Shai put the remaining food away.

"Did you talk to him?"

"I've ignored all his calls, Tara. Not planning on picking up. I told him like I told you two. He made his choice." Her sister had a soft blue apron on over her outfit, making her look even cuter and more pixie like.

"I liked him. I know you did. We are sorry it didn't work out."

She put her hands in the hot water, grateful to be inside, instead of out in that weather. "I'm sorry, too, but when I think about it, I got the goal I was after." A swift glance ensured her folks weren't around. "It was all about sex after all and I got more than that week."

Her sisters laughed.

"That's the truth and from the slow way you're walking when we saw you with him here, means you were getting a hell of a lot of that." Shai tossed the empty container at her. "Unless you're into something else you haven't been telling us about."

Eva blushed and shook her head. "Don't even go there. All it was between us was sex. A lot of it and good sex." Her brain burned with that lie. She'd gotten to know him and he her. At least, she thought she had.

"Good?"

She side-eyed Tara. "Yes, good."

"I bet it was way beyond good. Surely, you can find a different word to use."

Her body heated up at the memories of her time with Grant. "I could, Tara, but I'm not, because I'm not discussing the sex I had with a man in the kitchen at our parents' house."

Her siblings snorted and began laughing. She joined in then they dropped it away and finished while talking about something neutral. Current work situations. They knew from previous experience that if they got out of control with their laughter, their parents would be in to find out what was going on, just like they'd done all through their growing up years. And this isn't something she wanted to explain to them.

There wasn't any way she was about to sit here and discuss how Grant had his cock shoved up inside her wet, needy pussy and made her weep in pleasure, all right here in this kitchen. Oh, hell, no, ain't nothing on this earth going to have her in the middle of that discussion. She'd prefer some root canals without any Novocain or perhaps a hernia surgery without any anesthesia.

The sisters all decided to crash at Tara's place, given it was the closest to their parents' place and with the weather they didn't need to be out driving for longer periods of time. They caravanned it to her apartment and Eva was ready to head for bed after she took a nice hot shower.

Tara had also decorated her place for Christmas in a gold-and-red theme. The fire was going strong in the hearth as Eva shrugged off her shoes and wriggled her toes in the thick rug before the flickering flames. "Looks great, Tara."

"Thanks. You two up for a drink and some gossip?"

Tired or not, she loved gossiping with her sisters. "Absolutely, just let me go grab a shower and change out of these clothes."

All of them had clothing at the other's places since they dropped in quite often and sometimes crashed there. Eva grabbed some sweats and a long-sleeve tee then snagged a shower, moaning in pleasure as the hot pellets pounded into her tense muscles. When she finished and dressed, she joined her sisters in the living room where warm toddies had been made and waited for her.

Fingers curved around the heavy Tinkerbell mug, she took a sip. Heavenly. "Perfect drink on a night like this," she commented, settling in on the sofa.

"Thank you. You do your Irish coffee well, I do toddies."

They both looked at Shai. "What? I do a lot of things well. I just don't feel the need to advertise it. But I understand you two, it's your one thing. Be proud."

Eva smacked her with a pillow and Shai screeched, moving her drink out of the way.

"Don't spill it, now! This is precious." Shai sucked the drops off her finger that had splashed over. Her brown eyes glinted in the firelight. "My precious, my precious," she laughed.

"You two," Tara said, shaking her head. "How are we on Mom and Dad's present?"

"All wrapped and secured at my place." Shai grew serious again. "So even if they come snooping, they won't find anything. I left a note in my phone about where I hid the damn thing because I didn't want to forget."

"Awesome. Who's doing breakfast on Christmas?" Eva put her attention on both sisters.

"I have that as well," Shai stated. "You two are on Christmas dinner."

Eva gulped. She and Tara could cook but it was a passion of Shai's.

Her sister understood the look and chuckled. "I'll be there if you need any help, don't worry. You know it ends up being all of us anyway."

That was true. "Does anything else need to be picked up for the meal?"

"I've gotten everything on the lists. I'll take it to Mom and Dad's Christmas Eve Day. Since none of us work, then we can start making things for Christmas Day meal if that is best."

Eva settled back into the sofa and listened to her sisters talk. She finished her toddy and began dozing off. When she woke later, she was alone, the fire still burned and she had a blanket draped over her. The mug she'd held was no longer there. The room was dark aside from the fire.

For a moment, she debated on getting up and heading to bed. *Fuck it, Tara's couch is so damn comfortable. I'll stay right here.* So she tugged up the blanket even more and snuggled back down, giving in to the need for more sleep.

When she woke the next morning, it was to the smell of breakfast cooking with her sisters talking and laughing quietly in Tara's kitchen. She listened to them for a short time, enjoying being with her family before she sat up slowly and rubbed her eyes.

"Breakfast is ready in five minutes," Shai announced.

"Get ready for work, then you can eat." This from Tara.

"Which one of us is the eldest?" she asked, standing.

"The one who opted not to sleep in a bed last night," Tara teased.

"I was comfortable and warm," she admitted.

"Go get changed." Shai accompanied her order with a gesture using the spoon in her hand.

"Yes, mother." Eva trotted back to the room she used while staying over and pulled out some clean scrubs. As she folded up the clothes, she slept in to take home and wash, her phone rang.

Reaching for it, she shook her head when she read the name on the screen. It was Grant's sister's number. *Not this morning, I'll not let this sway my day. Today will be a good day. Today will be fine. I am stronger than this and I will survive.*

Pep talk over, phone call ignored, she went to eat, then headed into work. She was determined to enjoy the holiday despite her disappointment of not being able to share the time with Grant. Along with the disappointment of cutting him out of her life permanently.

* * * *

Grant grumbled as he made it through customs. He had disembarked from a flight from hell. Delays, massive turbulence, screaming children, vomiting people—hell, his shoes had to be thrown out. They were not going into his car. He was more than capable of driving home in socks. He didn't feel his clothing to be much better.

In the parking garage, he opened the back, tossed his bags in then swiped the extra pair of footwear he always carried. Once he'd exchanged them, he tossed the ruined pair in the trash.

Behind the wheel, he closed his eyes and took a few breaths, embracing the silence. And the lack of up and down sharp movement. Exhaustion heavy on his shoulders, Grant longed to claim his bed and sleep for a few days. After a nice hot shower, of course.

But he couldn't and he accepted the reason being a certain woman in Iowa who'd turned his life upside down. A female who epitomized sexy to him and made him want nothing more than to be with her.

Yeah, you showed that so well when you bailed on Christmas.

Okay, so his subconscious should shut the fuck up.

He licked his lips and put the keys in the ignition. Iowa and Arizona weren't exactly neighbors, so he had a while before he could see her. Technically, he had to be back to work in three days.

With a sigh, he turned off the ignition and climbed out before swiping his carryon that had another change of clothing within it and jogged back inside, beelining it for the ticket counter.

"I need to book a flight to Iowa please." He coughed and provided the city he wanted.

"Soonest flight I have leaves in two hours," the perky redhead behind the counter told him with a smile that appeared painted on her face, it never wavered.

Grant dug deep and scrounged up one in return. "Thank you, I'll take it."

He'd changed into some clean clothes but still wanted good sleep and a hot shower.

"Preference?"

"First class, please." At least there he could stretch out a bit and sleep on the flight.

She set him up efficiently and he soon had his boarding pass in hand, as he strode toward security. Grateful for the short lines, he didn't take long to get past their and to his gate, bringing his irritation down a few notches.

Sliding into a hard, plastic seat, he deposited his carryon between his feet and leaned back. A quick glance to his watch informed him of how much time he had until boarding. He struggled to stay awake while waiting and didn't dally when they called them up.

He declined any drink and just opened his blanket and covered up with it then propped his head up with a pillow. Then he went to sleep.

While it was utterly amazing what a few hours of sleep could do for a person, it wasn't nearly enough. He woke during the descent and didn't tarry in disembarking. Fingers flexing around the handles of his bag, he hastened to the exit and shivered at the cold.

Didn't think this through the clearest. In Uruguay, then back to Arizona. Now I show up where it's covered with snow on the ground and more coming down. Dressed in clothing for a warm climate. Fuck, it's cold here.

Hailing a taxi, he got in the warm vehicle and shared the address. The city was beautiful at night and he would have taken a bit more time to enjoy it but the need to see Eva gnawed at him and he hated how the taxi appeared to be driving up a molasses-covered hill.

Her place was dark and he hopped out. "Wait here for a moment," he said to the driver.

If she were at the hospital, he would be heading there next. Jogging to the door, he tried the bell. Three times. There wasn't any sound from behind the wood. No movement, no lights, nothing.

Cursing, he wheeled around and went back to the taxi. Giving the hospital as his next destination, he again occupied the backseat.

This, too, was a dead end as she wasn't working. He crossed his arms and thought about where she may be. Her parents' place? Grant wasn't keen on showing up there this time of night. Shai wouldn't be in her office but there was a chance that Tara would still be at hers.

So he headed there. Escorted up by security, he fought a yawn, walked along the darkened hall and paused before the door while the man with him knocked.

"Come on in," Tara called out.

"Don't stay too long now, Ms. Monroe," the man beside him stated as he waved him in the office.

"You know me, Marcus. Here until the job is done." She looked up and while the smile never slipped, Grant witnessed the change in her eyes, the warmth vanished from them, leaving behind what he assumed to be the woman people got to face in court.

Grant waited, not all that patient while they finished chatting and he exited the room, so it was just the two them, alone.

Those black eyes watched him with no emotion. The pink bangs didn't soften her appearance and he would never accuse her of being welcoming. "What are you doing here, Mr. Harrison?"

"Looking for your sister. She wasn't at the hospital nor her place."

Tara reclined back in her chair, eyes assessing and damning. "Let me get this straight, make sure I have all the facts. You were supposed to come be with her over Christmas, yet instead of being a man about it, you ran out of the country and didn't call her until after you'd landed in Uruguay. During which point there wasn't really anything further for you to say, aside from how sorry you were." She leaned forward, hands clasped on her smooth desktop, fingers laced. "What the hell makes you think I would help you find her and not have you thrown in jail?"

He drew back slightly. "Jail? For what?"

"Whatever charge I want to trump up on you." She spread her hands over the desk. "You hurt my sister. Made her cry. I don't like you."

"I know what I did was wrong. May I sit?" He waited a few seconds before taking a chair, even though she never nodded her agreement. "I was a pussy and I hid from my feelings. I want to explain this to her and move on."

"You expected her to what? Just wait for you to come to your senses? In case you haven't noticed, Doctor, my sister is a damn fine catch. It's not like there aren't other men who would be happy to have her in their life. Besides, she's moved on from you."

His gut soured at her words, but he maintained his blank expression.

Tara didn't let up. "In fact, for all I know, she's in bed with someone right now, enjoying his —"

"I get it." The words rolled from his mouth on a growl. He didn't need to hear this at all. Bad enough he hadn't been able to be with her over Christmas but to hear her sister speak as if she were already with another man. That was torture on an entirely different level. Again, nothing he could, or would, let her in on because given her expression, she'd only want to rub it in further.

"Do you? Really? She's not going to take you back."

"Yes." He longed to yell but contained his tone. "I get your point. She could be with someone else."

"And happy. She could be happy." She shifted in her seat. "That's the most important part of it all. My sister's happiness."

"I get it." His tone got sharper. He frowned again. "Why won't she take me back?"

She quirked an eyebrow. "Wanted to make sure you understood. I don't like you, Grant. You hurt my sister. Had her believing in you and how you were going to treat her right. She had fallen in love with you and you, what did you do? You broke her heart. Now that would be enough of a reason but there's more."

His head snapped up. "She loves me?"

"I said she'd fallen in love with you, not that she still was in love with you. Not that it matters, she won't allow you back in."

The hell she won't and what is the more, she didn't tell me? Yeah, he got that, but he was holding on to the fact she'd fallen in love with him. "Where is she, Tara?"

"I'm sure you think that doctor tone will get you what you want, and for some it may. Trouble is, I have a sister who's a doctor, and I'm used to the tone. Plus, I have one who teaches for a living and she is a master at that no-nonsense tone, so stuff it away, you don't intimidate me."

"I have no desire to intimidate you. I want to know where Eva is, so I can talk to her."

Tara leaned back and watched him with flat black eyes. "I want you to understand the only reason I'm telling you anything about her is because I saw how hurt she was when you blew her off."

"I didn't blow her off."

She snorted and shook her head. "Bullshit. You could have told her you were leaving the country well before you did, not calling once you there. That's blowing her off and not truly pertinent to this discussion. I'm talking to you, and if you're smart, you will be listening."

Grant ground his jaw but held his silence. She had the right of it, now wasn't the time to nitpick over the wording of what he'd done. He needed her on his side to dispense with the information he sought.

"She's down in Orlando."

"For?"

"Does it matter?" Condemnation lined her tone.

"No, it doesn't."

Tara picked up a sheet of paper and wrote something down then slid it over the desk to him. "I hear you hurt her again and I swear I will make you pay."

"An assistant district attorney making idle threats?"

Her black eyebrow jacked up and her gaze would have made sucking on icicles feel like drinking some hot coffee. She partially rose from her seat and nailed him to the seat with nothing more than a glare. "Trust me, this is no idle threat. Yes, I'm an ADA but first and foremost, I'm a sister and I hate the fact you've hurt my sister."

"Everything okay here, Ms. Monroe?"

Grant turned and saw that same security guard in the doorway.

"We're fine, Marcus," she replied. "He was just leaving."

Snapping up the paper, he didn't even bother looking at it, just got to his feet and shoved it in his pocket. "Thank you."

"Thank me by doing the right thing. Leave her alone after you say whatever you have to get off your chest. Let her get on with her life." She dropped her gaze to the papers in front of her making it very clear that he was no longer wanted in the office.

Holding his bag in hand, he strode out toward the waiting elevator. He passed a man approaching, dressed in a suit he knew cost more than anything he had in his closet. The impeccably clad dark-haired man raked his cold gray gaze over him then dismissed him without a second look as he flicked an imaginary piece of lint off his dark gray suit.

Grant didn't care whether the man was rude or not. He had a woman to track down. *I'm coming for you, Eva.*

Chapter Twelve

"Oh, God, that feels so good," Eva moaned.

"Glad you're enjoying my touch."

Her lips quirked as she tried not to smile. "Trust me, I most definitely am." Another deep moan slid from her throat as she allowed her head to fall forward further, giving him even more access.

"You know if you move here, we would be able to do this all the time."

Her body had no more stability than a quavering mass of a Jell-O tower. "So you're telling me to give up living in Iowa and move down here to Florida so I can be pampered like this?"

His fingers dug into her skin, working the muscles. "Hell, yes, that's exactly what I'm telling you. What the hell do you want to be there for, anyway? It's snowing there. Look at it here, we're in the seventies."

"You keep this up and we could be fifty below and I wouldn't care."

He laughed. "I would. Don't know how effective I would be wearing three parkas."

"Three? Most wear one."

"Sweetheart, look at me. I'm not exactly built for hardy weather like that. I'm the kind of man who needs sun, not snow. The whole less is more thing, not more is necessary for survival."

Joe moved down her back and she wanted nothing more than to sink into the chair and never climb out.

"You're way too tense," he said.

"I have to get back to work." Her words were soft and slightly slurred as she tried to wrap her mind around stopping this massage. It wasn't working and she didn't really give a damn. This man's touch was incredible and she wanted to allow him to finish the massage.

"You need to be on my table, so I can truly work this out for you. Come by tonight after work and I'll give you a massage. A proper one."

With great reluctance, she stood as his touch fell away. "Damn, you're good." She turned to peer at Joe. He matched her in height, but his hands were a gift from the heavens. Eva had no idea how he had gotten so strong.

He watched her with his black gaze, his tan skin showcasing his Asian heritage. "I know." His smirk was arrogant.

"And so modest, too."

"What's there to be modest about? I'm very good at my job. Now, I expect you at my table no later than six."

Her body was on board with that demand. Hell, it hadn't wanted to leave the chair for that impromptu shoulder massage he'd provided her. She swiped her stethoscope from the back of the nearby chair and draped it around her neck. "I will be there. And thank you."

"It's for purely selfish reasons. I want you to stay here in Florida. I like you and so does the staff and children."

"I love it here, but I miss my own kids. Plus, my sisters."

"Yes, but we're better and your sisters can come visit. Not to mention, you would grow to love the children here."

She rolled her eyes, blew him a kiss and left the lounge to head back to the room where she was giving a lecture. Their break had finished and it was time to work once more. She thought about it. Joe had made some good points. The weather was so much nicer down here. She couldn't deny the difference in her attitude down here. However, she hadn't lied, it wasn't easy for her to be without her sisters.

Their weekly get-togethers with just the three of them to catch up. Even the weekly family dinners she missed. And hell, she'd only missed one of them.

Eva smiled at a few of the people she passed by to get to the front of the room. Not much later and she was deep into her talk, thoughts of living here in the back of her mind. Everything but the information she was sharing was shoved away, no matter how temporarily.

By six, she was in Joe's room laid out on his table. The lights were low and he had some aromatherapy candles burning. Eucalyptus and patchouli scents were rich in the air, helping her remain calm and alleviate her stress. Granted, so did the massage she currently received. The thick towel over her ass the only thing covered at the moment.

The subtle mixture of jasmine, ylang-ylang and lavender filled the air mixing with the candle scents as he poured some oil into his hands.

"So, how did the rest of your talk go?"

Her lids fluttered closed as he began to work on her back. "Really well. We got a lot accomplished today. A few more talks and I will have nothing more to share."

"That, I doubt. Has Mr. Quintero tried to get you to stay as well?"

"He has mentioned it a few times."

"You know you should just give in and move here."

Her response was a grunt—it wasn't the easiest thing in the world to formulate responses when his touch was shot-putting her into a near catatonic state. The man had been gifted with magic hands, that's all there was to it.

Her phone rang and in her euphoric state, she fumbled for it to answer. "Hello?"

"You're not supposed to be on the phone while with me, sweetheart." Joe's comment wound around her as she waited for the person on the other end to speak.

"Hello?" she asked once more.

Still no answer, so she dropped the phone to her bag and yawned, burrowing deeper into the comfortable support she rested on.

"Who was that?"

"Beats me, they didn't say anything."

"They knew better than to interrupt us."

"You have no lacking in your confidence, Joe. I see this now."

"It's taken you this long to figure that out?"

"Maybe I was hoping it was all a trick of the mind. How do the kids put up with you?"

"They love me." He worked a particularly nasty knot in her lower back.

"Oh, God, that feels so damn good. Don't stop. Yes, right there, right there!"

"This is why I'm cocky," he said. "I know precisely how damn good I am."

"No arguments here." If she had the energy, she'd wipe the drool from her chin. But she didn't, and so it remained there.

They talked off and on for the remainder of her massage. When he finished, Eva had convinced herself she was nothing more than a pile of goo. Warm goo that just wanted to lie there and do nothing.

However, it wouldn't do to spend the night sleeping on his massage table. Joe left her alone and she slipped back into her clothing. He knocked then entered once more as she tied on her shoes.

"Are you sure I don't owe you for this?"

"Of course, you don't. I'm here to help sway you to stay here. I don't want you to head back this weekend."

She hugged him briefly and kissed his cheek. "I'll miss you, too, Joe." Eva exited the room and made her way down the silent hall. Her phone buzzed again and she checked the screen this time.

"What's up, Cynthia?" she asked, answering the phone to speak with the woman who manned the front desk at the hospital.

"I'm sorry to bother you, Dr. Monroe, but there's a man here to see you. Can I tell him a time that you'll be back?"

"I'm actually still here, Cynthia. I haven't left yet. Give me a few minutes and I'll be right there."

"Sure thing, I'll tell him to wait."

"Did he say what it was in regard to?"

"No. Won't say anything other than he wants to see and speak to you."

"On my way down." Phone shoved back in her pocket, she stepped into the elevator and pressed the button for the first floor. She scratched the back of her neck. "Not a lot of people know I'm here. Wonder who it could be waiting for me?"

With another yawn and a readjustment on her bag, she entered the open layout of the lobby. Smiling at Cynthia, she dropped her bag by her feet. "Hey."

"Hi, Dr. Monroe. You look so much better."

"Oh, my God, Joe's hands are amazing. Have you had that experience?"

She blushed and nodded. "I know—he could be so rich if he knew how to charge for his services." Clearing her throat, she gestured with her pencil. "Your guest is sitting over there. Or he was. Maybe he left."

"I didn't leave."

Eva's heart quadrupled in speed at that deep voice floating over her skin, setting it ablaze with a passion and need, only he could create.

Grant Harrison.

She angled her body toward that decadent temptation and found herself staring into his blue gaze. "Grant," she breathed.

"Hello, Eva."

How the ever-loving fuck he made two simple words like that sound akin sex handed to her on a velvet blanket, she had no idea. All she knew was he'd come for her. Whatever the reason, he'd come for her.

* * * *

Grant stared down at the woman standing in front of him. Her skin glowed and had a shine to it. Correction, she had a shine to her. He wasn't sure that change didn't have something to do with this man, Joe, and the hands they were talking about. Biting back his jealousy, he weighed his words to make sure he didn't fuck this up again, before he got a chance to make it better. "Eva."

She scrunched up her face, creating that cute wrinkle between her eyes. Dammit, he wanted to kiss her. Fisting one hand, he made sure to hold his ground. Not give in to his base urges. The most important thing would be to explain his situation and figure out how to move forward. Together, as a couple. Convince her that they had something to fight for, that there was a future for them to have and not alone, but with each other.

"What are you doing here?"

And there it was. The edge in her voice. The one hiding the pain and maybe even humiliation at how he'd treated her. He didn't focus on it, he couldn't or there wouldn't be any progress. "I thought we should talk. And since you didn't seem inclined to take my calls, I figured I would come to you."

"How'd you know where to find me?"

He debated lying for a moment but realized she and her sisters talked all the time. "Tara."

"That bitch."

"Everything okay, Dr. Monroe?"

Grant held her gaze and waited for her to answer the woman behind the desk.

"Yes, I'm fine. I need to talk to him for a moment." She handed over her bag. "I'll be back for that in a few minutes."

"No problem. Let me know if I should call security."

She gave Cynthia a smile and stepped away, so they could have some privacy.

"Why don't you just have her call Joe?" *Okay, that wasn't supposed to happen. I wasn't supposed to be attacking her, but being calm and not acting like a jealous asshole.*

"While I'm not sure where you got Joe's name from, you're wrong if you think he would need to rescue me. He doesn't need to rescue me. I'm more than capable of taking care of myself. And for the talking, well, I tried that remember, over Christmas? You were the one who didn't seem inclined to do any of that. So don't stroll in here thinking you have any say over what I do or who I may be doing it with."

The thread holding his calm in check snapped faster than a free faller careening toward the earth. He snatched her close to him, so close when he breathed in, her chest rubbed against him. "I know about Joe because I called you and was trying to get my nerves up to talk to you when you thought you'd hung up the phone. I listened to you talking and flirting with him and the moaning that came from your rendezvous with him." Bitterness tinged each word he forced out from behind clenched teeth.

Her skin flushed but he wasn't sure it wasn't from anger, or embarrassment. Perhaps a little bit of both.

"Eavesdropping should be beneath you."

"Nothing is when it comes to you, Eva. Who is he to you?"

"He's a masseuse. Nothing more to me, again, not that you have any say if he was more."

"That's where you're wrong."

Her eyes narrowed but she didn't pull away, he took that as a good sign. However, neither did she move closer to him. Since he couldn't read her expression, he wasn't sure what to make of that.

"How do you figure I'm the one in the wrong?"

"Because I have a fuck lot more to say if that man is more to you than a friend. As it is, I want to plow my fist into his face."

"How doctorly of you." Her words fell humorless from her lips.

"I messed up." He raked a hand through his hair. "No, let me correct that and call it what it truly was. I fucked up. I get that, Eva. But I'm here to fix my mistake."

"A mistake? That's what this boils down to you as? A mistake? Like one you can fix with flowers and a good fuck?"

He flushed, that had been his first thought.

She snorted. "Thought so. Listen to me, Grant, 'I want things when I want them and not a second sooner' Harrison. I don't work that way. I don't have time for little boy games. I thought you were a man who could talk about things, thought you wouldn't use some damn excuse to avoid coming to my house for the holidays. But you did. So I'll tell you what. Pretend you didn't find me here, pretend you came and there was some excuse waiting for you, I don't know, like, I'm out of the country, and you take your ass back to Arizona or wherever the fuck you're supposed to be right now and forget we ever met. It's like I said on the phone. It won't work. It never was going to. We don't work."

Eva wrenched away from him and walked off. She didn't stomp, didn't scuffle her feet, just walked as if she didn't have a care in the world.

As if he didn't mean a damn thing to her happiness.

For a moment, he stood there frozen to the spot as his brain tried to make sense of what just occurred. Then he shook it off and went after her. Catching up to her outside, he whirled her back to him and didn't give her a chance to say a single word. He slanted his mouth over hers and kissed her.

During those next few seconds, he wasn't sure if she was going to slap him but when she tilted her head to the side and moaned in the back of her throat, he knew her decision. Her tongue slipped to meet his as she wound her arms around his neck, pressing tight to him once more.

Where she belonged.

His joy was short-lived as she broke free and stepped back. "Don't do that again."

In the light of the parking lot, he could see her dilated pupils and chest heaving from her breathing. At her side, her fists were clenched and she moved her feet, as if she were unable to hold still. Torn between fight or flight.

He yanked his gaze back to hers. "Why not?"

"Because that's a privilege you no longer have. Goodbye, Grant."

He captured her wrist, trying to focus on the need to talk and not the pleasure he had from experiencing her smooth skin beneath his touch once more.

When he didn't release her, she cocked an eyebrow. "Are you going to make me call security?"

"We need to talk, Eva."

"Why? You made your point perfectly clear. Move on. I did."

Those words nearly killed him and he took a deep breath. "I can't."

"Not that I care, why can't you?"

He moved his thumb in small circles on her inner wrist. "Please, can we go somewhere aside from the parking lot to talk?"

"Fine. You can come to my hotel, but this is just for talking. I'm not fucking you."

"What happens will be entirely up to you."

She narrowed her gaze once more, but he didn't elaborate on that statement. If she changed her mind, he sure as hell wasn't going to pipe up and state they had to stop because of something said in a hospital parking lot.

Eva jerked from his hold. "I'm over here."

He trailed her to a small sedan and held his tongue as they got inside. As she drove, he remained silent, taking the opportunity to update his mental recognition of this woman. Her hair was a bit longer, still maintaining the blue tips. They were darker, so he wondered if she'd had them redone since he'd seen her last.

Still, his woman was sexy as sin and he wanted to strip away those scrubs and relearn everything she had to offer. From her posture, he didn't believe that would be an option for a while.

I really fucked this up.

She parked at the hotel and got out without speaking. He followed her in and to the elevator where she pushed the button for the tenth floor. As they ascended, he watched as she rubbed the back of her neck with a shake of her head.

They were in her hotel room within moments and he gazed around while she dropped her purse on the small table and the bag she carried on the chair next to that.

Eva kicked a chair in his direction. "So talk."

He gripped the back of the chair prior to claiming a seat. "What about you?"

Another yawn. "Look, I had a serious glow going on before you walked back into my life. My stress had been wiped away, now I'm tense and exhausted. Say what you need to say, so I can shower and climb into that very uncomfortable bed over there."

Ignoring the pain her words caused him, he nodded. "I was scared."

Nothing like being blunt but the time for me to dick around with excuses is over. I'm going to have to be honest with her if I want a shot at keeping her in my life. He didn't talk feelings. He didn't do this type of thing and it made him over-the-top uncomfortable, but for the woman in the room with him, he'd do this and more. Although walking barefoot over hot coals would be preferable to sharing feelings, he would find a way to get through it.

"Scared of what?" There was no condemnation in her tone this time, she was just asking for more clarification to his statement.

"Where we were going and what may happen if you decided you no longer wanted to be there with me."

"So instead, you decide to have me make all these plans for spending Christmas with my family and myself, then you call me once you're out of the country. Couldn't do it before you left the country, no, had to wait until after you landed in South America."

"I handled it shitty, no argument."

"You're right, no argument here for that shit you pulled. I spent the whole time telling my parents you had to work, making you out to be a great person."

"And your sisters?"

"Oh, they knew the truth of you being an asshole, which is why I'm surprised Tara told you where I was."

"She didn't just tell me where you were, she also threatened me."

"Tara's good at that. And she meant every word of it."

He swore her lips turned up a bit when she said it. This time, he ran both hands through his hair. Exhaustion had long since ceased nipping at his heels, it had started gnawing on his leg. He fought of another yawn, determined to make this right before he crashed. At least, he could acquire a room here. "I wanted to be there, Eva. Believe me."

"Hard to believe that when you bailed. And let's not call it anything other than what it was. You chickened out and didn't show."

He nodded. "I know I did. I ruined your reason to trust me. What do I have to do to get that back? I want what we had. No, that's not correct. I want more than what we had."

"I don't know, Grant. It seems you showed me what you were made of when you handled this before. I can't go through that again. It hurt and I've moved on." She sighed. "Besides, it's better this way. It wouldn't have worked."

No, he didn't want to hear this. He couldn't lose her. "Why do you say that?"

Her eyes shuttered before they appeared to calm and be damn near emotionless. She couldn't quite hide it all.

"I can't have children, Grant. I'm guessing you'll want someone who can carry on your family line. That's not me. You asked me back in Mexico why I got into what I am, and I only told you part of the reason. The rest is this. Because I had cancer. I'm one of the few who survived but not without sacrifices. I'm sterile. I can never swell with a child of my own. I won't ever know the joy of bringing life into this world. And I'm not going to put anyone else through that. So there…now you know the ugly truth."

Holy shit, that wasn't anything at all what he was expecting. Shutting his eyes for a moment, he opened them and pushed to his feet, stalking to her and sweeping her up in his arms.

"Grant, put me down." Eva struggled.

He ignored her slightly breathless command and carried her to the bed where he placed her with care down then joined her. Hooking his leg over her hip, he anchored them together. Grant rested his head against hers and sighed as her scent wove around him, calming the demons that had been alive and raging within him since his stupidity. He held her in silence for about ten minutes.

Eva didn't struggle, didn't argue about how tight he held her, just lay there, her arms between them.

Grant cleared his throat. "I'm in love with you, Eva Monroe. I know you're not going to believe me but it's the truth. I want to be with you. Marry you. If you can't have babies, we can adopt or be without. That doesn't change how I feel about you. We can do Doctors Without Borders if you'd like or something similar. I'll move to Iowa, whatever it takes." There wasn't any response from her, so he drew back a little and glanced at her. Her eyes were closed, her blonde lashes settled against her skin.

He shook his head, realizing she'd fallen asleep in his arms. "Figures the one moment I have the stones to open up to her, she sleeps through it."

Grant wrapped her up tight, ensured that they had no light between them, and despite his own exhaustion, took the time to enjoy having her back in his arms.

Chapter Thirteen

One second, she danced in her dreams the next — she dropped into reality and woke with a start. Eva's heart thundered in her chest as the strong masculine arms around her tightened.

What the hell is going on?

With caution opening her eyes, her heart slowed as she stared at Grant sleeping right there in front of her. He had his arms about her, keeping them tight together but he wasn't awake. Dark shadows underlined his eyes and he appeared gaunter than when she'd last seen him.

How could it be that this man could make her mad enough to spit fire but continue to make her heart go pitter-patter? All he had to do was look at her, caress her with his gaze and she was nothing more than mush. Didn't matter what he'd done. She wanted to forgive him, wanted to have him back in her life, so she could find that joy, that euphoria she'd experienced while being with him.

So why don't I forgive him? I've done things in my life I wasn't proud of. I've needed to be forgiven a time or two for my actions. And what the hell was I thinking to spit that out about being sterile?

Eva nibbled on her lower lip as she reached out to touch his face, lightly brushing her fingertips along his cheek. His stubble brought that familiar need within her belly. She loved how it brushed against her skin. His features had been memorized after all the time she'd been with him in person, then she'd also stared at any of the numerous pictures she'd taken with him. She knew his face so well.

Especially when it was between my legs or over me.

He'd come after her. All this time and she thought he'd left her life forever. Now, he lay here with her. Holding her like he had no desire to let her go.

Well, he may not want to, but her bladder currently screamed at her. So she wriggled out of his hold and went into the bathroom to take care of her needs. Before heading back out to the main part of the room, she turned on the shower and jumped in, just for a quick pick me up.

Towel wrapped around her, she stepped back out into the area of the hotel room where the bed was. Grant had woken up and lay there, eyes glued to the door.

"Morning," she said.

"Eva." He reached out a hand and beckoned to her.

"I have to get ready to head to the hospital, Grant. I can't do this. Not right now. I'm sorry I fell asleep last night but I'm exhausted." She pointed at his face. "From the looks of things, so are you. Get some more rest, we can talk later this afternoon when I'm finished with my presentation."

"I thought you were pissed with me."

"Oh, I am. Make no mistake about that but if we're both exhausted, nothing is going to come of it aside from yelling and accusations. We're both better than that." She checked the time on the clock by the bed. "But I have to get going so I'm not late."

"What are you doing down here?" He sat and the sheet slid down exposing his rock-hard chest and abdominals.

She bit back a whimper of need. "Sharing some procedures we do at our hospital with our patients. They're trying to improve on what they do and asked me to come down and share some of our practices."

"You're always willing to help out others."

She gave a small, easy shrug. "If I wasn't, I sure picked the wrong profession."

His grin did wicked things to her insides. Made her long to forget going in and hell, made her want to ignore the need for clothing. What harm would it do if she dropped the towel? Where would it lead?

"Come here," he ordered, sliding to the edge of the bed.

She listened then paused. "When did you take off your shirt?"

"Don't recall. Come here." He wriggled his fingers at her.

She took his hand and didn't speak as he drew her between his legs. Behind the cotton of the towel, her nipples hardened. This wasn't fair. Correction—this was downright torture. For her to be there, that close to him with only a towel between his hands and her body, was a level of temptation she wasn't sure she'd survive.

"I told you something last night, Eva. But you'd already crashed and didn't hear me." He took her other hand, lacing their fingers together. "I will tell you again, but I want to make sure you know something first, before you head out today."

She didn't even have to dip her head to look at him, he was right there, eyes on hers. "And what's that?"

Releasing her hands, he smoothed his over her sides and down to settle on her waist. He flexed his fingers, gracing along the curve of her hip.

"Grant?"

"I know I fucked up. I took the trust you'd put in me and shattered it. I will make it up to you. I'm not letting you go. I will find a way to fix this and earn that trust back. Get you back."

His tone wasn't cocky or condescending but heartfelt and dare she think it, honest. Her gaze softened and she sighed heavily. "It's not going to be that easy."

"Nothing worth a damn ever is easy. And you are worth it to me."

"Words are easy to spew forth, Grant. Actions speak so much louder."

His expression was crestfallen, and she had to harden her heart to the emotions that threatened to take away her resolve to not fall for him a second time. "I know they do. I'll make it up to you, Eva."

"I have to go."

He cupped her face and pressed his lips to hers, slipping his tongue into her mouth and twining it along hers.

She whimpered and sank her fingers into his hair, pushing harder against him. The she broke the breathless kiss. "I really have to go." If the repeat was to remind him or herself, she wasn't positive. Because all she truly wanted to do was have him pull away the towel and touch her like he had when they were together.

"If that's what you wish," he muttered, loosening the tuck of her towel. "God, I missed this. Looking at you naked. The smooth satiny skin that covers your fucking amazing curves. Your breasts that I can suck on forever and never get bored." His touch moved to over her belly, spreading wide, hovering above her pussy.

Her legs trembled and she locked her knees, determined not to collapse.

"Then there's this." He brushed his fingertips over the small triangle of hair she kept trimmed. "You're not bald here and I'm glad. I love this tiny patch of hair that leads me to your pussy. A place that cradles my cock unlike anything else I've ever experienced. A place that I love to lap and taste your cream as you come hard, thighs holding my ears as I'm between your legs." Grant leaned his head forward and flicked his tongue along a nipple.

His words brought images to her mind that she'd fought hard to suppress. His voice made her shiver and she knew she was drenched. She shuddered and he moved to another one, doing the same thing, causing the same reaction. Damn him and the way he made her feel.

"God, I want to feel you around my dick as I fuck you. Want to suck on your tits as you're riding me. I want to have your lips around my cock as I thrust deep into your throat."

She whimpered as cream gathered and leaked down her inner thigh. He cupped her pussy and she widened her stance, wishing for his fingers deep inside her. More of a touch.

"Tell me you missed me," he ordered, flicking his touch along her clit.

Her breath came in short rapid pants. "Yes, I missed you. Please, stop torturing me."

"You said you had to get to work." His words moved along her skin with his warm breath.

"I—I do." She shifted her hips, desperate to have him push his fingers inside her. Eva gripped his hair, tightened her hold and pulled. "Grant." His name fell like a plea from her lips. She took hold of his wrist and maneuvered his fingers to inside her pussy. "There. I need you there."

"Demanding," he whispered.

"Then why are you resisting?" Shit, she longed to feel his thick digits spreading her open, filling her, preparing her to accept his cock.

"Waiting for you to ask nicely."

"Is that so?" She dragged her fingers along his torso before maneuvering to the fly of his pants. "Or were you waiting for me to release your cock for you, straddle your lap and take you inside me, one inch at a time?"

"You're the boss," he replied. "I'm here to serve you. You state you have to get to work, yet here you remain, my fingers just barely brushing your pussy. I feel your cream teasing me, I know you're wet, I know how much you want my fingers deep inside you. I know you want me to fuck you. But I will not, not until you ask nicely."

She lowered the zipper and took him out, never once removing her gaze from his. His blue eyes deepened in hue, showing her a shade she only saw during high points of passion between them. It heightened her pleasure and she wanted the rest that came along with the privilege. Holding him in her hand had her near purring with pleasure. She stroked him as she stepped closer. "Then consider this," she said, moving over his legs to straddle him and line the head of his cock up to her core. "Consider this my asking nicely." She swiped his large head over her wetness a few times before lowering herself to accept him inside her heat.

"Fuck," he growled, dropping his hands to grip her hips.

She moved closer with this urge to climb inside his skin strong, she had to be up against him as close as she could. "Asking you, Grant, I'm asking you very, very nicely, to please fuck me." Her statement ended when her lips were millimeters away from his.

She knew the second he gave in, his growl rumbled up from his chest to surround her, followed quickly by his arms. "You ask so beautifully. I have no choice but to oblige."

His thickness pushed into her, reawakening every cell that had been sleeping since their last sexual encounter. Her moan filled the room as she tipped her head back, capturing her lower lip in her teeth. Blood heating, she looped her arms around his neck. She would deal with the aftermath later.

Right now, she wanted, needed, this. Something only he could provide for her.

Their mouths met in a flurry of increasing need and she gave herself over to the craving he created in her. The one only this man created within her.

* * * *

Grant gazed at the woman lying beside him in the hotel bed. Eva was a tiny pixie whose light sparkled the world on a scale that boarded massive. Her effect on people blew his mind. Adults and children alike, she got to them all and infected them with her spirit and heart.

She hadn't gone into work, she took a moment and called in to say she had to reschedule for later that she wasn't feeling that well. That had led them back to bed and more sex.

He wasn't going to disagree with that decision. However, he needed to speak to the woman in bed with him. While he stroked one finger down the middle of her back, it bumped over each disc in her spine until he stopped at the top of her ass. "Eva."

She stirred, rolling to her side and opening her eyes. "What?"

"It's time we talked."

Her sigh preceded her climbing off the bed and tugging on her shirt. "So talk."

He bit back his moan of disappointment when she shimmed into her pants moments later. "Come back and sit."

"Put your pants on." The words fell from her lips as an order.

He nodded and tugged them on before he sat back on the bed and beckoned her to join him.

While Eva didn't take his hand, she did sit on the bed, crossed her legs, and waited for him to say something.

"I made a mistake," he admitted, taking her hand in his. "My decision to not come be with you over the Christmas holiday will haunt me for years to come. I wanted to be with you, but I was scared. I can admit that. Worse than that, I was a coward."

She stared at him, her blue eyes remaining without any emotion in them.

"No comment?"

"No need for me to make one, I agree with you. You were a coward."

A brief smile turned up his lips. "Of course, you wouldn't argue that."

"Did you think I was going to make it easy on you?"

"Kind of hoped what we just shared would have earned me a bit of leeway."

She yawned behind her small hand. "Sex wasn't an issue between us. We burned up the sheets without any problem. That's been the case since we first fucked in Mexico. We were discussing your problem with commitment."

His chest grew tight but he ignored it. If he wanted to keep this woman in his life, he had to face his feelings. "I want to be with you, Eva. More than I ever wanted to be with anyone. I began feeling that the moment we met. Each second I spent with you, it grew stronger, never once weakening."

She swallowed and tilted her head to the side. "So you're saying that despite how much, how strong you wanted to be with me, when it came time for something as simple as a holiday meal, all your desires to be with me vanished without the simplest of trouble? Not only that, for whatever reason it made you not want to tell me you weren't coming until you left the country? I can see how strong this desire is."

He coughed to cover his uncertainty. "Sarcasm deserved, I get that. But no, it wasn't that simple. And it still kills me how I handled that situation."

"You didn't handle it," she admonished. "You ran."

"I did. Not proud of that. But I'm here now. Christ, Eva. I got off the flight back and immediately booked another one to Iowa, where I landed and went to your house then the hospital to find you. They wouldn't give me anything, so I tracked down Tara, who I figured would still be at work. After she gave me a piece of her mind, she told me to come here and find you. So I did. I'm trying to make up for it." His frustration grew, as her expression remained unchanged. Unimpressed with all the sacrifices he'd currently made. But it wasn't only directed at her, this was an issue he'd brought upon himself because he'd been unable to face his feelings.

Her silence filled the room.

"So, that's my reasoning for what I did. Tell me what I have to do, what I have to say to get us past this. I heard you about not being able to have children, I don't care."

Eva shrugged. "I don't know if there is a way beyond it. I don't forgive easily." She rose, shaking her head. "I need to get to the hospital. I'm sorry, Grant. Sorry you came all this way for nothing."

He sat there in disbelief as she backed away from him and put on her shoes. "So that's it? You're just going to walk away from what we have?"

"We don't have anything. We had something, not anymore." She brushed her hands down her clothing and took a deep breath before staring at him once more.

He read it in her eyes even prior to her saying another word. This was it for her. Unable, or unwilling, to hear it pass her lips, he leapt from the bed and lifted her in his arms, moving until the wall stopped his forward progress. "No," he barked out.

"No?" Honest confusion filled her expression. "No, what?"

"I'm not letting you give up on us that easily."

Tears sprung to her eyes. "You think this was easy for me? Easy to give my heart and have you rip it free and stomp on it?" The tears never fell and the sadness segued into anger.

Her agony tore at him, yet he refused to release her gaze. His cock rested against her core and he wanted nothing more than to sink it into her heat. There was no arguing when they made love. There was only pleasure. Only happiness. Only bliss. Perfection.

"I'm right here, Eva, handing you mine. Giving you my heart. But more than that, I'm asking you to trust me with yours once more."

"To what end?" She hooked her legs around his waist, tighter. There wasn't any way to deny the hope in her tone, the wistfulness.

Still, he couldn't ignore the fear and he knew that was because she was scared to trust him again. Scared he would hurt her again. "Marriage, growing old together. Lots and lots of sex." He'd meant it in a teasing way that last sentence but didn't even receive the barest hint of a smile.

"Is that what this is supposed to be?"

"What this are you talking about?" He lifted his eyebrows.

"Is this blathering you're doing right now supposed to be proposal?"

He swallowed hard. "No, this isn't a proposal. When that happens, I promise it will be done right."

"Sure, it will." There could be no denying the doubt in her tone.

He pushed into her, flexing his hips to rub his cock along the seam of her pants.

Her lips parted with a sigh and she rocked back.

"Focus, Eva. As much as I want to fuck you again, not happening until we get this cleared up."

"Then finish it up, so I can go."

"No, we're not rushing just because you don't want to discuss that I want a life with you."

She dragged her nails along his neck, skyrocketing his pulse. "You want a life with me? Want me to believe that this was more than a fling, that if you'd come to Christmas we would somehow be in a different place in what our relationship used to be? Prove it."

"I have nothing else to prove, Eva. I'm here, for you…that should be proof enough."

"You were supposed to be here for Christmas."

He clasped a hand around her neck and leaned in, so his lips nearly brushed hers. "You are frustrating and so fucking stubborn. I'm here, I came for you."

"And when you decide to leave? Are you going to tell me before or will I just wake up to find you gone without any note?"

"I'm not leaving you again. Yes, I have to go back to Arizona, but I'll do that to move to Iowa. Or here, if you're wanting to be in Florida."

Her eyes widened.

Finally, he was getting through. He nodded. "You heard me right. I can't live without you in my life anymore. So if it takes me moving to be with you, so be it. I'll move. I can work at a different hospital."

She held the wrist of his hand he had on her neck. "Put me down."

The fuck he wanted to do that, but he listened to her, continuing to keep her trapped between him and the wall behind her.

"Why did you wait so long to tell me this?"

"So long? I've been trying to get to you since before Christmas. You wouldn't take any of my calls. My entire flight back was figuring out how to get you to answer me. My sister tried to call you and there wasn't anything there either from you in the way of picking up the phone."

"No, I didn't want to talk to her."

He swiped his thumb along her lower lip. "I don't want to play games, Eva. I want my ring on your finger."

Looking troubled, she started shaking her head.

Grant gripped her chin. "No. No more excuses. I love you. I'm in love with you. We don't have to get married right now. I'll get you an engagement ring, whatever you want, just give us a chance. You grabbed me from the first. And the more time we spent together, the deeper I fell. When you showed up at my father's funeral and I asked you why, your answer was so simple, so heartfelt. You told me it was because I needed you. And you were right. I did then, and I do now."

Silence again. Torturing and seemingly infinite silence shouted at him. It stretched to a full minute but to him, it felt like days as moisture pooled in her beautiful eyes. What else could he say or do? She was going to shoot him down. She wasn't—

A smile peeked at the corners of her lips, then she kissed the pad of his thumb. "Just so you know, I want a killer engagement ring." Her statement was accompanied by a full smile as her gaze softened.

Relief flooded him as even he knew his heartbeat had reached an unhealthy pace. He lowered his head and kissed her. Then when he pulled away, he felt the tears in his own eyes. "You can have whatever type of ring you want. I love you, Eva."

"I love you, too, Grant." She wound her arms back around him and sank into him. "Now, I really have to go in and do my presentation."

"I'll be here when you come back."

"Good, because I have some work for you to do." Her hand covered his dick and gave a light squeeze.

"We'll be ready."

The moment she left the hotel room, Grant sat on the bed and released the longest, most heartfelt sigh ever in his life. He just sat and stared off into space for an indeterminate amount of time. He'd thought she was going to walk away, and he felt like death had come to his soul. He'd never been good at emotional talk, but he used up a lifetime's worth today.

He snapped out of it and knowing he must be the luckiest man on earth, he called his mother then his sister, letting them know the news. After which, he settled in to figure out what he was going to do, if they ended up in Iowa.

Chapter Fourteen

"Are you sure about this, Eva?"

She glanced over her shoulder to stare at the vase Grant held up for her. Tall at about twenty inches, and pale blue and rose-colored glass. "No." She chuckled at his expression.

"So put it into your third 'maybe' pile?" he asked.

Eva scuffed her toe on the carpet. "Yes. And I think you may just be exaggerating a bit if you are claiming this is my third 'maybe' pile."

"Oh, no, definitely I am not. The first was there by the bay window. The second was behind the couch. Now if I'm doing this one, it will be here, by the hearth."

"It was a gift," she pouted.

"Everything in here is a gift from someone or another. The question is do you want to take them all with you? And I'm fine if you do, just would like to know one way or the other, so we can either pack them away or put them in that small pile of donations."

"What do you expect? I've lived here my entire life." She faced the wall, determined not to start crying again. There would be enough of that when her sisters arrived this evening. She didn't need to be doing that now. Not when she had tons of work to accomplish. It was just so damn hard.

He slid his arms around her from behind and pressed a tender kiss to the side of her neck. "I know this is hard for you. You grew up here, went to school here, and have been practicing your entire career here."

Eva rested against him, settling her hands over his where they lay on her belly. "I know, plus I haven't been away from my family like this."

"I told you we could have stayed here. I would have moved."

"I know but your mom isn't doing the best, and with your sister having a baby, it's best if we are there to help take care of her when it's needed."

"You always think of other people. Do you ever put yourself first?" He whispered the question along the shell of her ear.

Her heart did so many pitter-patters she was shocked he'd not heard any of it or seen that organ trying its best to escape from her chest. "I do. I'll have you know I'm a very selfish and greedy person when it comes to sharing you."

Grant tightened his hold and nuzzled her neck, his scruff abrading along her sensitive skin. "That isn't something you will have to worry about. Unless it's my mom."

"I know." She closed her eyes as he ran his thumb over the engagement ring on her finger. They'd been engaged for eight months now and he'd wanted to move in together. She was on board with that. This long-distance thing was damn near killing her.

"Are you sure you want to move to Arizona?"

"Of course, I'm not sure. My whole family is here. But I think it will be for the best. I'm excited to be going to the new hospital and they have some new procedures out there I'm looking forward to learning about so I can implement them."

He moved his hands down below the waistband of her pants, keeping along the outside of her thighs but it didn't matter. His touch was a powerful aphrodisiac to her, it created within her such longing, such need. Her nipples pebbled and drew tight behind her bra. Her clit pulsed and she rubbed her legs together in a futile attempt to stem the craving for his caresses.

"Have I told you today how fucking sexy you are?"

"No."

"Are you sure?" He moved his hands in wide circles on her legs.

"I'm dressed in sweats and a raggedy tank. Sweating and cursing. Sexy is not a word I would use to describe me at all."

"You don't have to. I will. Hell, fuck that. I am using that very word. I love how you approach life, Eva. Everything is an adventure. Everything can be fun if you are surrounded with the right people and the right attitude. Like right now, I know you're sad, I know you're fighting back tears because you're leaving your family. Yet through it all, you still effervesce. I can't explain it. However, I will tell you that this sweats and tank top look works for you. Especially with the way it clings to your body. How the sweats curve around your ass and the tank highlights my breasts."

She laughed and nudged him. "These are not yours. I'm pretty sure these are my breasts."

He used a hand to pull her top away from her chest and peered down the front where he made some grunts and moans. "Nope." He turned her in his embrace, so they were face to face. "These are mine."

She flashed a grin. "You have your own."

"Trust me, Eva. I don't want to play with the ones on my body. I want to play with yours."

"See, now you got it right, these are mine."

He growled and snapped his teeth at her. "No." Grant covered them with his hands. "Mine. See how they are straining into my touch?"

She took one of his wrists and guided him down the front of her body until he cupped her core. "This is straining for your touch. So stop making it beg."

He rubbed along the seam of her sweats.

It wasn't nearly effective enough but regardless it was better than not having him do anything to her.

"Is this mine, as well?"

She rocked against him, desperate for increased friction. "Yes." The word fell from her lips on a sigh.

"So it's all mine." He dipped his head and flicked his tongue along the whorl of her ear. "All of it is mine. Tell me."

"And if I do?" Her body rebelled against her putting any sort of hesitation on its relief. She needed to have him grinding on her clit, bringing her to orgasm.

"Then I will reward you by giving you what I know you want."

God, his voice, his words, pure temptation to sin and in the most decadent of ways. She trembled and dug her fingers into the side of his shirt, gathering it tightly. "Can't you just give it to me, anyway?"

"I could but I'm not going to, not until you tell me what I want to hear. Not until you agree with what I'd said about this being mine." Back and forth, he moved his hand.

His touch and hold on her had pretty much relaxed her legs to the state he was just mostly supporting her weight. "Yours." The word was almost inaudible.

"What was that?" He sucked on her neck.

Eva had no doubt she would have a mark there tomorrow. "I said it's yours. All of it. Me, breasts, pussy. All yours."

"And your heart?"

"Definitely yours."

He slid his hand down the front of her pants and edged the panties over, allowing his fingers to tease the lips.

She gasped and widened her legs. "More," she begged.

"Trust me, baby, there will be so much more." He pushed his finger deep into her, the cream from her slit making it glide without pause.

"Yes," she cried, dropping her head backward to rest on his chest. "Fuck yes."

"Take your shirt off," he ordered.

Eva didn't hesitate, just whipped it over her head and tossed it somewhere. She wasn't wearing a bra, hated the things and never wore them at home if she could get away with it.

Grant lifted his head and stared at her before dropping his gaze. "Such a beautiful sight. Just the same as when I first saw it in Mexico." She squealed as he lifted her with one arm. Grant moved them to the wall and he put it at her back. Pushing another finger into her, he pistoned them in and out while he claimed her mouth. When she came hard around his fingers, he pulled them free and dragged them over her nipples.

Eva held her breath as he flicked out his tongue and cleaned off the moisture he'd just applied. "I love how you taste." Light teasing laps until there was no more of her essence on her tips, then he used harder, firmer swipes.

She loved how he loved it. Closing her eyes, she just enjoyed his ministrations on her body. They started at the wall then moved.

When she woke up hours later, they were curled up in the bedding on the floor of her bedroom, naked and limbs intertwined. There was sound out in her living room and she groaned, realizing that her sisters had already arrived and were waiting for them to emerge.

This is going to be one hell of a night. Lots of being picked on, I'm sure.

* * * *

"You going to take care of her, correct?"

Grant glanced down at Tara, the tiniest of the three Monroe sisters. She barely hit five feet, but he wouldn't challenge her any day. She would easily be classified as a pit bull who was hungry and wanted the bone in your hand. "Of course."

She stared up at him with those almond-shaped eyes. The black color fathomless and he couldn't read her expression. "The jury is still out on you, Grant. You hurt her once and she took you back. Do it again, you'll never come back."

He outweighed this woman by a good buck-twenty, easy. Hell, he wasn't even sure she topped the scales at one hundred pounds. But she delivered this ultimatum and threat without blinking an eye. "Another threat. I got it the first time. I don't want to hurt her."

"First off, this isn't another threat. Hell, it's not even one. This is a promise. She's our big sister and we protect our own."

"I'm going to be family. Doesn't that award me any leeway?" He gave her a smile.

Her gaze narrowed slightly before she recovered. "No, marrying into the family doesn't mean a damn thing. You have to prove yourself."

"Understood."

She pivoted to walk away and he cleared his throat, causing her to turn back. Grant hesitated for not much more than a second before took the chance, grabbed her close and hugged her. "I love you, little sister." Then he let her go.

"You smell nice."

He blinked, fully having expected a knee to the groin or a punch to the head. That sentence wasn't at all what he thought would have been coming from her. "Thank you."

Shai moved by and stopped, flicking her glance between the two of them. "What's going on here?"

Tara jerked her thumb at him. "He smells nice."

"And for this, we ignore how much he hurt her?" Shai crossed her arms.

"No, not ignore, sis, but reevaluate. Smell him."

"No, I'm not smelling him. I'm going to pack some more boxes." She walked away before he could hug her, too.

It was well past ten at night when he stood by the fireplace and watched as Eva hugged her family. Even her parents had come by and this was the final farewell.

Tears flowed from everyone, even her father. Now it was just the sisters.

They stood together, arms around one another in a three-way hug. He couldn't make out what they were whispering to but the words would be unknown to him even if he could hear them. The bond between them so powerful, it didn't matter they weren't of the same blood. He'd never seen a stronger or closer group of sisters.

In the back of his mind, he had trouble reconciling the fact he was taking her away from this. From them.

Just then, Eva lifted her head and speared him with those damnable blue eyes of hers. Through the tears, she smiled and he knew in that moment, all was okay with her. She didn't have a problem leaving with him. Perhaps it would be better to say she wouldn't be holding it against him later on down the road. The love in her gaze wasn't anything he could miss.

Sure, she would miss them, and sure, times may be hard but they would face it together. He blew her a kiss and stepped back, allowing them the time and space they required to say their farewells. Grant had no desire to rush her, he would allow her to take all the time she needed. This was going to be hard for her. This family was so close.

He waited for her in the bedroom when she finally made her way there and wordlessly opened her arms for him to walk into them. Rubbing her back, he dropped a kiss on the top of her head.

"I'm going to miss them so much."

"I know you are, sweetie, but it's across the country, not the world. We'll see them more than you think."

She rubbed her eyes on his shirt and sniffed. "I hope so."

Tipping up her face so he could see her eyes, he rubbed his thumb along the bottom of her lip. "What can I do?"

"Just hold me. I need you right now to just hold me."

Grant scooped her up and carried her to the bed. A bed that in a few hours would be broken down and in a truck. Lying beside her, he allowed her to get as close as she wanted.

Eva slid her hands beneath the cotton of his shirt and ran her palms up his torso. Then she wedged her legs between his, burrowed a bit closer and sighed.

He locked his cock up in the 'need to behave' zone and threw away the key. She needed him to be there for her, not to get all randy and fuck her. Even so, he couldn't help his physical response to her. He brushed his cheek against her hair, reveling in the softness. Arms tight around her, he closed his eyes and listened to her breathing. One of the most important sounds in the world to him.

"I love you," she muttered before she fell asleep.

"Love you, too," he said once her breathing had evened out and she'd fallen under the lure of the sandman.

It had been a busy day and after she'd been asleep for a while, he would go back and finish the rest of the packing that had yet to happen, allowing her to continue resting.

Epilogue

Arizona
Two years later

"Your wife is on the line, Dr. Harrison."

He popped the final carrot stick into his mouth and jogged to the phone hanging on the wall. "Thanks, Cara." He smiled at the blonde woman at the front desk.

Picking up the receiver, he said, "Hey, baby. Everything okay?"

"I'm fine. Sorry to bother you at work." Eva's sultry voice flowed out and around him.

"You could have called my cell phone, you know."

"Don't have the number memorized and your niece is chewing on my phone currently. I don't think your sister is feeding her kid."

Grant laughed. "Tired already?"

She muttered something he was sure he wasn't supposed to hear. "This isn't funny. Your sister didn't

189

say this child was like the Energizer bunny who refuses to nap or even slow down."

"I know she appreciates you helping her out."

"I love your sister. It's her spawn I'm having issues with."

"I don't hear any screaming or crying."

"I told you, she's chewing on my phone. It's when I try to take it away from her that the screaming and crying start." A deep sigh. "Anyway, before I lost my only form of viable communication, I had a call from Tara. She wants us to come to Switzerland for the Christmas holiday."

"Sounds like fun, but I hear a hesitation in your voice. What's wrong? Don't you think we can both get away at that time?"

"That's not the issue."

"Then what is?" He frowned and hooked his foot around a chair, dragging it closer to the phone.

"Well, that's nearly nine months away."

"Works well that way, given we're in March."

"Smart ass."

"What's going on, Eva?"

"How do you feel about dual citizenship?"

He rubbed the back of his neck. "I'm not following. Are you planning on moving to Switzerland? Is this why you're asking?"

"No. God, I suck at this. Okay, here we go. I'm due the twenty-seventh of December."

"Due for what?"

Silence reigned.

His world shrank and he swore all he heard was the thudding of his own heart. "Are you saying what I think you're saying?" He licked his lips more than once and did his best to build up some moisture within his mouth, which felt like a cotton field.

"Yes." Her tone vibrated, light and unsure.

"And you're telling me this while I'm here? Instead of at home with you?" The room spun. How the hell had she handled this, it had to have been a shock given her belief it wouldn't be able to happen.

"I was there earlier. You were in surgery. I didn't want someone else to spill it to you and I know you're there overnight."

"I'm going to be a daddy?" Fuck, his heart wouldn't stop pounding, his hands were sweating and he really had this urge to bend at the waist and put his head between his knees, just to try to catch his breath. Regardless, that option may not work at all.

"Yes."

"I'm coming home." He had to be with her.

"No, work your shift. We'll celebrate when you come home. But I have to figure out what to tell Tara."

"How about this, we go earlier in the year. That way, you can still see, her but we don't have to worry about you being close to term." His heart pounded in his chest. *Christ, I am going to be a father.* Was it okay if he hyperventilated? His head swam with the news. He had to find out how much of a risk she was going to be and guarantee that he did everything to make sure that this baby was not miscarried, or that he lost her.

"I'll let her know. I'll see you in the morning."

"Yes, you will. You most definitely will." He closed his eyes and got to his feet. "I love you, Eva."

"I know you do, Grant. I love you, too." She hung up the phone, leaving him with nothing more than the dial tone.

His smile nearly cracked his face as he replaced the receiver and stepped away. Still a bit lightheaded, he replaced the chair and leaned against his locker.

"All good, Harrison?"

He cracked an eye to see fellow surgeon, Dalton Rogers standing there. "Fine. Wife just told me we're expecting our first."

The man's dark face widened as his smile made his teeth shine bright against his skin. "Congratulations! That's wonderful news. I've got five of the little rugrats. They're each amazing."

"Not sure if we'll hit five, but I'm damn sure excited about this one."

Dalton nodded. "It will only get better. Was that why she was here today?"

He cocked a brow at the man.

"You know my Lucinda works down in the lab."

"That's right. Okay, I have to go make rounds. Have a great night."

"You, too, and again, congrats."

Sliding on his white coat over his scrubs, Grant stepped out of the lounge area, full of joy and hope for the future. The night passed relatively quick, and as he drove home, he grew more and more antsy with each passing mile. One never knew about the human body. Being a doctor had taught him this. It was pronounced years ago that Eva would never be able to have children, but yet again, the human body surprised him. Or was it love that had done it? He beamed like an idiot while driving alone in his car, grinning hugely the entire way.

Daylight had yet to crest the horizon as he parked in the garage to their apartment building. He loved Arizona. Honestly, he'd been shocked when Eva had told him she didn't have an issue moving all the way out here to be closer to his mom. She'd thrived while being out here. He watched her while being outdoors a lot more. She enjoyed the weather and loved the fact her winters were not spent bundled up, looking something akin to an Eskimo.

He climbed up to their apartment on the third floor and put his key in the lock, his smile still glued to his lips. Opening the door, he found the place still dark. He placed his keys on the end table, toed off his shoes and padded to the bedroom.

She lay there, sleeping on her side, one soft warm light the only illumination while it filled the air with subtle scents of lavender and light amber.

Grant perched on the edge of the bed and reached out a hand, stroking it down the side of her face.

Eva stirred and opened her eyes. "Hey," she said with a smile.

He dipped his head and brushed his lips along hers. "Hey, yourself."

She inched over and patted the mattress beside her.

Grant removed his clothing and slid beneath the sheets, wrapping her in his arms. With her body pressed tight to his, he groaned and smoothed his hands down her back, anchoring them together. He nipped the whorl of her ear and kissed her.

"How was work?"

"It was fine. I don't want to talk about that."

Her slender shoulders moved as she shrugged. Eva still didn't look up at him, just kept her face against his chest. "Can we sleep a bit more?"

He inched his fingers down farther, along the curve of her ass, until he hit the back of her thigh. "You want to sleep?"

Her laughter pumped more life into his blood. His cock stiffened and throbbed.

"I could do with a few more hours. I was on the phone most of the night with family letting them know the news." She curved her fingers around his cock. "However, I think there is something else I would be more than happy to do. I can sleep later. I have the day off."

He bucked his hips, groaning again at the feel of his length moving along her palm. "So, then, we're sleeping later?"

She inched down along his body. "Later," she agreed, and replaced her hand with her mouth.

As her tongue swiped over the crown and head of his dick, he squeezed his eyes shut. God, he loved this woman. They would talk later about the baby. Right now, his thoughts were focused on one thing and one thing only.

Grant had what he needed, his wife and a baby on the way. A dream that strolled in along a beach had made his life complete. "Yes, I need you now, Sweet Eva."

Want to see more from this author? Here's a taster for you to enjoy!

Temporary Home

Aliyah Burke

Excerpt

"Get the hell out of here, you mangy, good-for-nothing kid! Don't let me catch you around here again."

Samuel Hoch went flying through the air only to land in a partially frozen puddle. Seconds later a splash sprayed his face with icy pellets.

"You do and you'll wish you were dead."

He already did. Sam scrambled towards his bag as the heavy door slammed behind him. The wintery wind swirled around, biting into his skin with vicious tenacity. Fighting back his tears, he tried to get up only to slip and fall again, this time wetting the rest of his thin and worn clothes.

It isn't fair. Why am I out here?

"Easy there, son."

Sam stared up in shock to find a tall black man standing there looking down at him. He took in the white hat with the black brim, the blue pants with a blood-red stripe on them—visible from beneath the dark coat — and the shiny shoes. He knew what he'd found. Or rather who had found him. A Marine.

The man extended his hand and it seemed that even the leather of his gloves was spotless.

"I'm fine," he snapped, embarrassed and a bit frustrated.

"No harm in accepting some help." The man's tone never changed. His deep bass rumbled, reminding him of thunder.

Sam reached out slowly, half expecting the hand to jerk away or hit him in the face. Neither happened, and the man lifted him clear of the freezing water with ease. Sam's teeth began to chatter as more of Minnesota's winter wind slammed into him.

"You have anywhere to stay tonight, son?"

Mute, he shook his head as the large man began shrugging out of his coat. Sam was in awe of the uniform and never even moved when the heavy coat was placed on his too-thin shoulders. Immediately he warmed as the wind was blocked. The sleeves were too long and they fell to drag on the snowy ground. All he could think about was how nice it was to no longer be freezing.

"Come on, son. Let's get you to some shelter for the night. Going to get right cold tonight."

He lifted his head and stared up at the imposing figure. If the wind or cold affected him, Sam couldn't tell. The man seemed unbothered by it all. He still hesitated — he'd seen what happened when boys went off with adult men. Those images and screams gave him nightmares.

"I have your things, come along."

He walked beside the now-silent Marine. His smaller steps were weighed down by the heaviness of the wool coat. He didn't mind the heat but he was exhausted and so hungry. At the end of the alley, the man paused and glanced down.

"Name's Dean Richardson."

"Sa...Sam Hoch." The words were painful sliding through cracked lips.

Dean turned left and walked again. "Nice to meet you, Sam."

That was it, all the man called Dean Richardson said as they walked along the snowy streets. It didn't take too long before they were walking up the steps to a large stone church. They didn't go in the front but headed around to the back. There Dean knocked.

Warmth and bright yellow light spilled out when the door was opened. An older man with silvered hair stood there.

"Dean. Good to see you."

"Thank you, Father. I brought someone who needs some help" — a pause — "at least for the night."

Kind blue eyes found him and soon Sam was welcomed inside. There were about fifteen other boys running around. They all halted in what they were doing and stared at him. He stepped closer to the tall Marine.

"We should have some dry clothes which will fit you. I'm Father Michaels, by the way."

"S...Sam." His teeth still chattered but he was not as cold as he'd been before.

Another gentle smile. "Come along, Sam. You'll feel better dry and with some food in you."

He peered up at Dean who gave an encouraging nod. "Go on, son."

He went and when he returned, Dean was still waiting. His coat, with its muddy and snowy hem, rested beside him on a second chair. His hat sat next to him on the table. Sam couldn't explain his relief at seeing him there. The man spoke to Father Michaels. The light gleamed off his shaved head, creating an even more imposing figure. Still, the brown eyes, which met his were soothing.

Dean approached, gestured him into a chair at the table then sat across from him. "You're going to be okay, son." He reached out his hand, a card extended from his fingers.

Sam took it and read the printed words. Staff Sergeant, Dean Richardson, United States Marine Corps. He didn't know what it all meant but he was glad to have it in his grip. There were also phone numbers on it.

"Work and home. You can call me any time, Sam."

He didn't know what to say and so just blurted something out. "I'm sorry about your coat."

Father Michaels set a plate of food in front of him before disappearing again.

A wide, brilliant grin. "Not to worry. A little dirt never hurt a coat." He got to his feet. "You're safe here, son. Father Michaels is a good man."

After stabbing some of the ham from his plate, he shoved it in his mouth. "Why did you —"

"Don't talk with your mouth full." Dean's reprimand was delivered in an authoritative yet calm voice.

He swallowed and tried again. "Why did you help me?"

"Everyone needs help at some point, Sam. Remember that." Dean walked off, slipping on his coat and holding his hat.

Sam watched the man speak with Father Michaels then open the door and step though, simultaneously placing his hat on his head. Then Dean Richardson was gone. And Sam again felt alone.

For the first night in over a month, Sam crawled into a bed, which wasn't made of collapsed cardboard boxes or on a heating grate. His bag of personal belongings was beside him as he snuggled beneath the warm blankets. In his hand he held Dean's card. Too exhausted to remain awake, and confident he was safe, at least for the moment, he succumbed to the sandman's irresistible lure.

"Sam!" a voice called. "Sam!"

Twenty-seven years later
Washington State

"Sam!"

He jerked and looked around. A dream, it had only been a daydream. Sam Hoch glanced down at the boy who'd fallen to the deck of the ferry. His mother—at least he assumed it was his mother—pregnant and with a harried expression on her chubby face, hastened to them as fast as she could.

"You okay, son?" he asked, reaching out to help the child up.

He nodded, accepting the assistance. "I was hiding from my mother. What's your name?"

His heart clenched at the innocence the boy had. What would a childhood like that have been like?

"I told you not to run on this ferry, Sam." The mother was out of breath and her expression was concerned.

"I was bored," the child whined.

Sam stood so the woman could have his seat. She accepted and sank heavily beside her now-pouting child. "Thank you," she said. "For helping him and for giving up your seat."

"Everyone needs help at some point." Sam walked away as Dean's words slid from his lips.

Dean. His mentor. His friend. And the man he'd thought of as his father. The reason he was on the ferry from Seattle to Bremerton. Dean was in hospital. He'd been diagnosed with bone cancer and had been undergoing chemo. It hadn't been going well lately and they'd had to stop the chemo and admit him, just to see if they could put some weight back on him and get him strong enough to endure the treatment again. It didn't look promising, though. Nausea churned in his gut at the thought of losing him.

Aside from the Corps, Dean Richardson and Dean's niece had been his only family.

"It is so like the commercial. This man is wearing the same thing."

Sam heard the not-so-hushed whispers behind him and continued to face forward. The boy he'd helped before. The one with the same name.

"You talked to him once, ask him." Another child spoke. "Or are you chicken?"

He knew what was coming. Sure enough, the little boy and his friend popped around him, both bundled up against the winter air off the water. One boy white and one Asian.

"Sir?"

"Can I help you boys?"

They shared a glance before a nudge was exchanged.

"Do you do like the commercial?"

He peered down, knowing that in his dress blues with blood stripes he looked the same as the Toys for Tots Marines on the television advertisement.

"Christmas is almost here," he said. "There's not much time left."

"I know. It's why we need to know."

Their expressions were so hopeful he was hard pressed not to smile. Beyond them he saw the pregnant woman again, her expression even more drawn and full of apology. He gave her a small nod before returning his attention to the boys.

They spoke of the toys they wanted, games and clothes. When the ferry docked at Bremerton, he stared at the boys before going down on one knee. "I'll see what I can do, but remember the most important thing is being with family and those who love you. Help your mom out."

He regained his feet and headed for his truck to disembark.

About the Author

Aliyah Burke is an avid reader and is never far from pen and paper (or the computer). She is married to a career military man, and they have a German Shepherd, two Borzois, and a DSH cat. Her days are spent sharing her time between work, writing, and dog training.

Aliyah loves to hear from readers. You can find her contact information, website details and author profile page at http://www.totallybound.com.

www.ingramcontent.com/pod-product-compliance
Lightning Source LLC
Chambersburg PA
CBHW020430180626
46812CB00003B/1168